KT-420-670

DONCASTER LIBRARY SERVICE

30122 03115938 3

# Get ready to be swept off your feet by perfect English gentlemen!

Mills & Boon® Romance
brings you another heartwarming read
by international bestselling author

## *Jessica Steele*

Jessica's classic love stories will whisk you
into a world of pure romantic excitement…

**Recent titles by this author:**

A MOST SUITABLE WIFE
VACANCY: A WIFE OF CONVENIENCE
PROMISE OF A FAMILY

**Jessica Steele is the much-loved author
of over eighty novels.**

Praise for some of Jessica's novels:

'Jessica Steele pens an unforgettable tale
filled with vivid, lively characters,
fabulous dialogue and a touching conflict.'
—*Romantic Times BOOKreviews*

'*A Professional Marriage* is a book to sit back
and enjoy on the days that you want to
bring joy to your heart and a smile to your face.
It is a definite feel-good book.'
—*www.writersunlimited.com*

'Jessica Steele pens a lovely romance…
with brilliant characters, charming scenes
and an endearing premise.'
—*Romantic Times BOOKreviews*

# THE BOSS AND
# HIS SECRETARY

BY
JESSICA STEELE

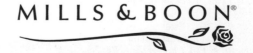

MILLS & BOON®

All the characters in this book have no existence outside the imagination of the author, and have no relation whatsoever to anyone bearing the same name or names. They are not even distantly inspired by any individual known or unknown to the author, and all the incidents are pure invention.

All Rights Reserved including the right of reproduction in whole or in part in any form. This edition is published by arrangement with Harlequin Enterprises II BV/S.à.r.l. The text of this publication or any part thereof may not be reproduced or transmitted in any form or by any means, electronic or mechanical, including photocopying, recording, storage in an information retrieval system, or otherwise, without the written permission of the publisher.

MILLS & BOON and MILLS & BOON with the Rose Device are registered trademarks of the publisher.

First published in Great Britain 2007
Harlequin Mills & Boon Limited,
Eton House, 18-24 Paradise Road, Richmond, Surrey TW9 1SR

© Jessica Steele 2007

ISBN-13: 978 0 263 19613 9
ISBN-10:    0 263 19613 5

| DONCASTER LIBRARY AND INFORMATION SERVICE | |
| --- | --- |
| 30122031159383 | |
| Bertrams | 01.04.07 |
| | £12.25 |
| | |

Set in Times Roman 9¾ or
07-0407-58919

Printed and bound in Great Britain
by Antony Rowe Ltd, Chippenham, Wiltshire

**Jessica Steele** lives in the county of Worcestershire, with her super husband, Peter, and their gorgeous Staffordshire bull terrier, Florence. And spare time is spent enjoying her three main hobbies: reading espionage novels, gardening (she has a great love of flowers), and playing golf. Any time left over is celebrated with her fourth hobby: shopping. Jessica has a sister and two brothers, and they all, with their spouses, often go on golfing holidays together. Having travelled to various places on the globe, researching backgrounds for her stories, there are many countries that she would like to revisit. Her most recent trip abroad was to Portugal, where she stayed in a lovely hotel, close to her all-time favorite golf course. Jessica had no idea of being a writer until one day Peter suggested she write a book. So she did. She has now written over eighty novels.

# CHAPTER ONE

TARYN was aware that her concentration had gone to pot and pulled in to the side of the road. Sitting in her parked car, she felt poleaxed by what she had just done—by what Brian Mellor had just done.

She had worked at Mellor Engineering for five years, and had grown to love Brian ever since she had been promoted to his PA two years ago. Brian was head of the prosperous and well-thought-of-company. He was a good employer and they worked well together. He was tall, blond, easygoing, kind—and married!

His wife, Angie, was a lovely person too. Not in features. In actual fact Angie Mellor was rather plain. But what she lacked in beauty she more than made up for in her quiet but warm and giving personality. It was clear that she adored her husband, clear also that their children, seven-year-old Ben and three-year-old Lilian, adored their father too.

That their marriage was blissfully happy was apparent to anyone who saw Brian and Angie Mellor together, which had greatly helped Taryn to keep her love for him hidden.

Disturbingly, though, she had sensed around six months ago that everything was not going so well in the Mellor household. Taryn had not been quite able to put her finger on what was wrong, or to know why she felt that anything *was* wrong. Just an out-of-kilter word here, a cross look there when Angie came into the office, which she did every Friday when she was in town shopping.

And then, two months ago, Angie had stopped coming in on a Friday. 'Is Angie all right?' Taryn had asked Brian on a number of Fridays.

'Fine,' he'd replied absently, and straight away plunged on with some work-related issue.

It had worried Taryn. She'd felt she knew Angie well enough to ring her on some pretext. But to do that somehow seemed to be not only prying but, since Brian had said his wife was 'fine', slightly underhand.

Matters appeared not to have not improved. And on that very day, Taryn, much to her own astonishment, let alone anyone else's, had walked out on her job!

Sitting motionless in her car, she could still not quite believe she had done what she had. She loved her job. She was good at it. She loved Brian, was fond of his wife—but having walked out, there was no going back. There could not be; she just knew it, no question.

Feeling shaken, and very much all over the place, Taryn relived how the day had started much the same as any other day. She had parked her car and made her way into the many-storeyed building that housed not only the head office of Mellor Engineering, but other highly successful companies too.

She'd been first in; she sometimes was. With her home life not as harmonious as she would have liked, she often left for work early, and, depending on what particular strife was taking place at home, frequently worked late.

When Brian had arrived that morning, however, he'd seemed a touch distracted. Taryn had made no comment but, having dealt with some of his post, discussed the remainder with him and then returned to her own office.

She'd watched him, though. Throughout that morning, whenever they'd been in contact, she had watched the man she'd only ever known as pleasant as, clearly unhappy about something, he went about his business.

But it had been nearing four that afternoon when she'd had cause to go into his office and, observing his strangely morose expression, had just had to softly ask, 'What is it, Brian?'

'Nothing…' he began. But then, sort of lunging to his feet, 'I've had enough,' he said in a strangled kind of way. 'I can't take any more!'

'Oh, Brian love,' she murmured, the small endearment, often thought but never said, out before she could stop it.

'Oh, Taryn,' he cried miserably, and before she had a clue to what he was about to do—almost as if he needed to hear some kind word, some hint of human caring—he took her in his arms.

And she was so shaken by the suddenness of it all that she just stood transfixed. She might, she realised, have instinctively held on to him. Whatever, he must have felt emboldened that she was not moving away, because the next she knew Brian was kissing her.

At first she still stood there, somewhere in her head knowing that he was distressed and in need of solace. But seconds later, as his hold on her tightened and his kiss became seeking and that of a would-be lover, so Taryn knew that it was not just a hug of comfort that this man wanted from her.

Shocked, bewildered, and even a little outraged—while at the same time a small voice within her urged her to give in, to yield to this man she loved—Taryn thought of Angie, the children and, while she still could, she pushed him away from her.

She didn't wait for what he would do next—apologise or kiss her again—but in blind panic, perhaps afraid of her own instincts, knew only that she must not let him kiss her again. Wildly she charged back to her own office, stayed only long enough to collect her shoulder bag and jacket and, all before Brian Mellor had recovered his breath, she was out of there.

The lift doors were just about to close as she reached it—she had been about to rush down the stairs. Tears were stinging her eyes as she sped into the lift—she was not aware she had company.

In fact the lift had begun to descend before she became fully aware that she was not alone. She doubted that, with her head in such a turmoil, she would have noticed that she was not the sole occupant, had not the other person present made some observation.

'You seem upset?' An all-male voice interrupted the turbulence of her thoughts.

Her deeply blue eyes shining with unshed tears, she glanced at the tall man who was somewhere in his mid-thirties. He was dark-haired, grey-eyed and, from the cut and quality of his suit, obviously successful.

'What?' she questioned, feeling irritated by him. Her glance fell away and she noticed abstractedly the expensive-looking briefcase in his hand. He had clearly been in the building attending some business meeting or other. Perhaps he worked there? Had an office in the building? She had not seen him there before anyhow. She dismissed him from her mind.

'Is it something I can help you with?' he persisted.

Give me strength! 'I very much doubt it!' she retorted jerkily, and was thankful that just then the lift came to a halt and she was able to end the unwanted conversation.

Taryn bolted from the lift and was in her car heading for home before she realised that she did not want to go home. Her retired scientist father was mainly in a world of his own, and might not think to enquire what she was doing home so early, but her stepmother, who only a few days ago had lost yet another housekeeper, would not only have a string of chores lined up for her—and another string of complaints—but would have a string of questions too. Sometimes—in actual fact quite often—Taryn found her stepmother hard to take.

Taryn suddenly realised she must have been sitting parked in her car for quite some while, as her agitated thoughts jumped around in her head. Gradually, though, she grew calmer, and began to recover from the shock of Brian Mellor kissing her the way he had.

While her thoughts were still in some sense of disarray, she began to ponder on her flight from Brian's arms. Perhaps it was the total unexpectedness of what had happened that had knocked her sideways? Should she have handled it differently? Could she in fact *have* handled it differently? Maybe.

Though, on thinking about it—and she had thought of little else since it had happened—what else could she have done but get out of there? Had she not loved Brian there might well have been a chance she could have given him a shove—along with a few choice words—and that would have been that.

But she did love him, and owned with painful honesty that when he had kissed her she had been on the verge of responding. And she, Taryn knew, would have found it impossible to live with that. How would she have been able to live with herself? How would she ever have been able to look Angie Mellor in the face again? Because, no matter what had gone wrong between Brian and Angie, they were still married and, Taryn was certain, still very much in love.

It did not make her feel any better to know that she had done the only thing she could have. But, as Taryn accepted she could not sit there much longer, she still did not want to go home.

She could, she supposed, go and have a cup of tea somewhere. But she did not want tea. She did not know what she wanted. Oh, why had Brian spoilt it all? While nothing especially exciting was happening in her life, she had been enjoying her job.

The word 'job' reminded her of her aunt's temping agency. Taryn and her aunt got on extremely well, and her aunt Hilary, her father's sister, ran Just Temps, not so very far from where she was.

On impulse Taryn took out her phone. 'Are you busy?' she asked. Her aunt had inherited the same workaholic streak that ran all the way through most of the Webster clan. Taryn herself had inherited it from her father.

Hilary Kiteley, as she now was, had been on her own since her husband had died some thirty years previously. Financially she'd had no need to work. But, because she had needed something challenging to fill her days, she had learned all she could about a business she had taken on and expanded, and which was now very well respected.

'You're not in your office?' Hilary asked.

'Can I come and see you?'

'My door is always open to you, Taryn, you know that.'

Half an hour later Taryn was sitting in her aunt's office, having explained that she had just walked out of a job which her aunt knew full well she had thoroughly enjoyed.

'Are you going to tell me what happened?' she asked gently.

Taryn shook her head. 'I—can't,' she replied, and loved her aunt the more that Hilary Kiteley did not pester to know—as Taryn knew her stepmother was going to—but smiled encouragingly.

'Perhaps, when you've had time to think about it, you'll go back?' she offered.

'I won't,' Taryn answered, and knew it for a fact. That kiss had changed everything. She loved him, and had been tempted. The risk of giving in was too great. He and Angie must sort out whatever crisis was going on in their marriage. They had to!

'Well, you're obviously very upset, whatever it was.' And, with a far more logical head than Taryn felt *she* had at the moment, 'Would you like me to find you something temporary while you sort out something more permanent?' Hilary Kiteley enquired.

What she would do next had not occurred to Taryn. She would get another job; it was in her nature to work. But she wasn't ready yet to be PA to someone other than Brian Mellor; she did not know when she would be.

'I don't know that I want to be a PA again,' she confided.

'You'd be good at anything you tackled.'

'Oh, Auntie, you always were good for my self-esteem.'

'With just cause! Remember that spell of waitressing you did for me when you were at college? They would have taken you on permanently, had you wished.'

As perhaps she had hoped, that comment drew forth a smile from her anguished niece. 'Perhaps I'll try waitressing again,' she said with an attempt at lightness. And, realising she had taken up enough of her aunt's time, 'I'd better be making tracks for home.'

'I hear Mrs Jennings left rather abruptly?' Hilary commented, referring to their last speedily departed housekeeper.

'You've been speaking to my father.'

'You're cook tonight, I take it?'

Taryn knew that she would be. Her stepmother was not much interested in food. And, even though she had at one time been their housekeeper, she was even less interested in matters domestic. If Taryn's father was to eat—and his own culinary skills came in the 'couldn't boil an egg' category—then it went without saying that his daughter had been elected.

'We'll get a replacement housekeeper soon,' Taryn said hopefully, and was grateful that her aunt did not state her opinion that her stepmother would be wasting her time applying to Just Temps for someone to fill in meanwhile.

Instead she asked about the much discussed issue. 'When are you going to leave home? You've been going to for years,' she reminded her.

'I know, and I really would like to move out. But every time I mention it something seems to go wrong at home.'

'Like the time your stepmother had a fall the night before you were due to move out? Like the next time you came home to find her with a bandaged foot and barely able to hobble about? Not forgetting the time she thought she needed an operation—only then discovered the problem had miraculously cured itself?'

'You've got a good memory.'

'Eva Webster may be your stepmother, but I've known her for longer,' Hilary stated, having known Eva Brown, as she had then been, for years.

She had known her long before Taryn's mother, a gentle soul, had decided she could no longer put up with her husband's long term neglect and, the day after Taryn's fifteenth birthday, had explained to her daughter that she had fallen out of love with Horace Webster and in love with someone else. She had left, and Eva Brown, a widow in reduced circumstances, had moved in—as housekeeper. The day she had married Horace Webster, however, was the day she had determined that her housekeeping days were over.

'That woman uses you like a skivvy,' Hilary Kiteley went on. 'And expects you to be grateful to be living under the same roof.'

Taryn, feeling a touch disloyal to Eva, even if her aunt was only telling the truth, did not answer. 'How's my favourite cousin?' she asked. 'Have you heard from Matt recently?'

'He's busy, but he manages to give me a call now and then.'

'Give him my love the next time he rings,' Taryn requested, and getting to her feet, 'I've taken up enough of your time.'

'Feeling better?' her aunt asked, going to the door with her.

'Much,' Taryn replied, but more from politeness than truth.

'Give it twenty-four hours and it will all seem so much better,' Hilary assured her.

Taryn drove home, wishing she could think so, only to garage her car and enter the large but cheerless house, and be greeted by her stepmother's demand of, 'What's going on?'

For a split moment Taryn wondered if her aunt had telephoned her stepmother, before instantly dismissing the notion. Aunt Hilary would not do that. 'Going on?' she queried, having arrived home at more or less a normal kind of time.

Somebody *had* been on the phone, she discovered, but not her aunt. 'Brian Mellor has rung twice, wanting to speak to you. He'd tried your mobile—you'd got it switched off.'

'So I had,' Taryn replied, vaguely remembering she had switched it off after her call to her aunt. She made a mental note to keep it switched off. She did not wish to speak to Brian. What was there to say?

'You'd better ring him. What does he want you for?'

'No idea. Have you made a start on dinner?'

'I had a migraine.'

Away from the subject she did not want to talk about, Taryn, after enquiring if her stepmother felt better, made her way to the kitchen.

Sleep did not come easily to her that night. She had loved that job, was comfortable with engineering and engineering terms, had computer and typing skills and, a quick learner, tackled anything that passed by her desk with enthusiasm. What sort of career did she have now?

Did she even want a career? She felt hurt, wounded, and had not replied to Brian's phone calls. She relived again the way he had kissed her. As such matters went—and she knew that she was behind the times in that regard—she was not so very experienced. But she knew the difference between a kiss of friendship and even a shade or two warmer type of kiss—but those sorts of kisses had been a mile and a half away from the kind of kiss Brian had given her.

Not that it had been so much 'given'. It had just sort of happened. She had been standing there, she had been empathetic, and then, *wham*, he was on his feet, kissing her—a kiss that had been all wanting. And she had panicked and had got out of there.

She'd been in the lift, having terminated her employment with Mellor Engineering without having to think about it, and… She suddenly remembered that man in the lift. Oh, heavens, had she been very rude to him?

Poor man… Oddly, she could see him quite clearly in her mind's eye. Tall and, if not concerned exactly, there had been something in his grey eyes as he'd asked—she had to think for a few seconds—'You seem upset?' and, 'Is it something I can help you with?' And she had snootily and quite snappily retorted, 'I very much doubt it.' Which, in the circumstance of him only wanting to help, had not been at all gracious of her.

Taryn put the picture of the good-looking, quite obviously top executive from her mind. She didn't know who he was, and if she ever did—which she wouldn't, because she was never going to enter that building again—she was unsure that she would want to resurrect what had happened by apologising for her rudeness.

She wondered what to tell her father and stepmother at breakfast the next morning. But was grateful that her father had an experiment going on in one of the workshops belonging to his property, and appeared to have forgotten the need for breakfast. Taryn thought she might take him a tray later. Her stepmother left it until after nine to descend the stairs.

'You still here?' she exclaimed, when they bumped into each other in the hall. Taryn was saved a reply when just then the telephone in the hall rang for attention and her stepmother reached for it. 'Hello?' she enquired. 'Brian!' she exclaimed, and, archly, 'Didn't that naughty stepdaughter of mine ring you?' Taryn made frantic signs that she still did not want to speak to him, and saw Eva hesitate before she declared, 'I'm sorry, Taryn's not around at the moment. Can I take a message for you?'

Apparently she could not. But the moment she put the phone down she wanted to know, chapter and verse, why he was ringing her stepdaughter at home when said stepdaughter was supposed to be in his offices.

'There was… I've resigned,' Taryn stated.

'A pity you didn't tell him that!'

'I'll drop him a note.'

'You've walked out!' It sounded like an accusation.

'I—um—wasn't sure I wanted to be a PA any more,' Taryn replied, feeling her colour rise at the blatant lie. Although, since she was not sure what she wanted to do any longer, perhaps it was not so very blatant.

She watched as her stepmother's need to know every last minute detail rose to a peak. Then all at once it fell away as Eva Webster fitted in her stepdaughter's lack of employment with a vacancy she had of her own. She seized the opportunity with both hands. 'Well, isn't that splendid? You can have Mrs Jennings' old job!'

'I'm—er—not sure I want to be housekeeper to you and Dad,' Taryn tried to protest.

Overruled. 'You're surely not thinking of sitting at home idle all day?' questioned that lady who had made sitting idle an artform.

Since Taryn did not want to spend the next week avoiding answering the phone—if that was how long it took for Brian to get the message that she was not going to go back, and assuming that was what his phone call had been about—Taryn that day typed out her formal resignation. She sighted unforeseen circumstances as her excuse to put on file for her departure being immediate.

By return she received a handwritten note from him, apologising profusely for overstepping the line between employer and PA, and stating that he had no excuse to offer other than the fact that he saw her in a more friendly light than someone who just happened to work for him. That, however, did not make his behaviour any the less inexcusable. But, while he could promise that nothing of the sort would ever happen again, if he had to he would accept that she would not be coming back. If at any time she had a change of heart, there would always be a job for her at Mellor Engineering.

Taryn had a hard time holding back tears as she read his letter. She felt she had never loved him more than just then. But she could not return. It hurt her not to see him. It hurt not to be a part of that busy environment. Being her stepmother's housekeeper just did not compare.

Taryn had been cooking and cleaning and generally putting up with her stepmother's daily demands for going on two weeks when she began to feel that they would be falling out 'big-time' if she had to put up with much more of it.

She was still missing going to work at Mellor Engineering every day—it was taking a little longer than the twenty-four hours her aunt had forecast it would take for it all to seem much better. But Taryn did admit to feeling more on an even keel as she searched through the 'Situations Vacant' column for something that might trigger a spark of interest.

'What dainty sandwiches are you preparing for this afternoon?' Eva Webster demanded on entering the room.

'Sandwiches?'

'My bridge party?'

It was the first Taryn had heard that her stepmother was entertaining her bridge chums.

'I thought salmon and cucumber, with a few little cakes afterwards,' Taryn replied off the top of her head—anything for a quiet life.

'White *and* brown bread?' Eva Webster demanded sharply.

'Naturally,' Taryn answered, realising she would have to go to the shops. Woe betide her if the bread wasn't fresh.

Her stepmother looked over Taryn's shoulder and was soon ready with her next demand. 'Why are you reading the "Situations Vacant" column?'

Taryn smiled. 'I'm looking for a job.' Eva Webster's lips compressed; she did not like it, but by no chance was Taryn going to allow her to believe she was going to act as housekeeper permanently.

'You obviously haven't got enough to do here,' Eva snapped, referring to the fact that Taryn, who had vacuumed and polished the morning away, was now sitting reading the paper.

Taryn switched from 'Situations Vacant' to 'Accommodation To Let" when she had gone. Perhaps this time she would not tell her stepmother her plans until, cases packed, she was on her way out of the door.

Taryn was returning from the shops when, feeling more than a little down she played with the notion of paying a visit to her mother. Her mother and new husband did voluntary work in Africa.

Would she be welcome, or would she be in the way? Her mother's letters were always warm and loving, but…

She had come to no decision when, her stepmother's bridge party in full swing, the telephone rang. Taryn answered it in the kitchen, and with a warm feeling heard her aunt's voice.

'What are you doing?' Hilary asked.

'In between looking in the "Situations Vacant" and "Accommodation To Let" columns, you mean?'

'As bad as that?'

'Not really,' Taryn answered. Her aunt loved her, she did not want her to worry about her. 'It's just me—I don't think I'm suited to this housekeeping lark.'

There was a slight pause, then, 'That's a pity,' her aunt was saying.

'It is?' Taryn queried.

And was soon informed, 'I've had a request to find a temporary housekeeper for two weeks. They want someone a little bit special—I thought of you.'

'Oh, Auntie —I'm flattered. Isn't that nice?'

'But you don't want it?' Hilary asked, going quickly on before she could reply, 'It would solve both your job and accommodation hunt for two weeks,' she reminded her. 'And you could still look out for a new job, and at the same time it would give you two weeks' breathing space from the dreaded Eva.'

Taryn had to smile. 'Oh, I don't know,' she murmured. But she had to admit that the prospect of another two weeks at her stepmother's beck and call had less appeal than that of taking on a similar job for someone else. There couldn't be two like Eva, could there? 'Who's it for?' she asked. 'And where?'

'It's for a lovely old gentleman living in the Herefordshire-Wales borders,' Hilary replied.

'You're sure he's a lovely old gentleman?'

'Positive. Would I send you anywhere not nice? His present housekeeper, Mrs Ellington, has just been on the phone to me—

it appears she was recommended to us by a friend of a friend, isn't that super? Anyhow, she has worked for Mr Osgood Compton for the last ten years and describes him as "a dear man", an octogenarian, and a true gentleman, apparently.'

Taryn had to own that she was warming to the idea. 'His housekeeper—Mrs Ellington—she's going on holiday?'

'She has a daughter who is unwell. She wants to go and spend a week or so with her, to gauge for herself if everything is being done that should be. It may be that you'll not need to stay the whole two weeks there,' Hilary said, and coaxed, 'In the circumstance of being so well-recommended, I should like to pull out all the stops.'

'Can I think about it?'

'He needs someone straight away.'

Thinking on the spot, it did not take much thinking about. Taryn had arranged to see some of her friends on Friday. They were mainly people she had met at college, with some added and others falling away. But she could easily cancel her side of the arrangement. And, to her mind, just two *days* away from her stepmother, let alone two weeks, would be a bonus. Taryn did not need to think any longer.

'You'd better give me his address,' she accepted.

'Wonderful!' Hilary exclaimed. 'When will you go?'

'Tomorrow,' Taryn answered before she should change her mind—but didn't look forward to telling her stepmother.

Taryn made her way down to the village of Knights Bromley the following morning. As she had anticipated, her stepmother was far from thrilled at the idea of having to do her own housekeeping. But, her word given to her aunt, no amount of pressure would make Taryn go back on her promise.

Mrs Ellington was there at the big old house to meet her when she arrived, and stayed long enough to go through the many notes she had thought to make, and to introduce Taryn to her temporary employer.

And Osgood Compton was, as Mrs Ellington had told her aunt, a true gentleman. Within hours of Mrs Ellington leaving, Taryn was feeling more and more at home.

By the time half a week had gone by she was feeling as relaxed and as if she had known him all her life. At the end of that week she felt it had been the most tranquil week she could ever remember. Osgood Compton was a sprightly gentleman, for all his eighty-two years, and with a lively mind to match.

Her duties for her new and temporary employer did not stop at housekeeping, however. Osgood Compton, albeit with the company of a walking stick, liked to walk. His walking stick was not his only companion on his mile-long expeditions either. And, as one week turned into two, Taryn would often look up from what she was involved with and find him standing in the doorway.

'Any chance of you dropping what you're doing?'

And Taryn had no problem at all in dropping what she was doing. So they walked and, since he liked to talk too, they chatted about all sorts of subjects. He had been an engineer of some note before his retirement, and seemed delighted that she knew the names and actions of the various engineering implements he mentioned.

In a very short space of time Taryn began to feel quite an affection for him, and knew she would look back on her time with him with pleasure when her two weeks were up.

But, as matters turned out, Mrs Ellington's daughter was diagnosed as requiring immediate surgery, and she rang Mr Compton to ask if he would mind if she had another four weeks off. He, of course, being the gentleman he was, told her to take as long as she needed.

'Dare I ask you to put up with me for another month?' he asked Taryn.

'I love it here,' she told him simply. 'Another month will be fine.'

'It will just be for one month, I promise,' he replied, and, with a beaming smile, 'Perhaps you'd better ring the agency and let them know?' he suggested.

Later that night Taryn heard him making his own phone call to his daughter, who was married to an American and lived in the States. He and his daughter were in fact in frequent telephone contact with each other, and Taryn felt it was a very loving relationship.

For a brief sad moment she wished that her father might show her a little more affection than he did. But that was not his way, and she soon brightened when, as she passed the open drawing room door, she heard Mr Compton telling his daughter of his good fortune in exchanging one gem of a housekeeper for an absolutely diamond one.

While Taryn felt that that was quite something of an over-the-top exaggeration, it nevertheless made her feel good to hear him say what he had.

Taryn later rang her home, and heard the joyous news that her stepmother had found a new housekeeper. From that Taryn guessed that there was no need for her to hurry back.

The weather over the following weeks was more often than not glorious, and, her temporary employer decreeing that it would be criminal to spend their days indoors, he urged Taryn to make picnics. She needed little urging—any chores that didn't get done during the day she could catch up on during the evening.

And so the days passed, which would see her scurrying around in the mornings and then taking leisurely strolls to some picnic spot. Occasionally they stopped to quench their thirst at the village pub and, on one most memorable time, even indulged in a game of darts. All in all, they spent some very pleasurable summer days.

As the end of her six weeks in Knights Bromley came to a close, Taryn was still of the view that she would not be going back to Mellor Engineering. But she now felt more ready to take on work in an office environment. She had needed this break, she realised. Had needed this time away in order to get herself back together again.

She must now think of making a career for herself. She was ready for it. She determined that the first thing she would do on

Monday morning would be to get down in earnest to finding that career job. The second, having had a respite from her cold and at times alien home, would be to find herself somewhere else to live.

Her determination to do either had to be put on hold for a while, she discovered, when the very next day Mrs Ellington rang to say that her daughter, although doing well, had taken a step backwards in her recovery and she was reluctant to leave her. 'Do you think you could stay on for another week or two?' she asked. 'I know Mr Compton thinks the world of you.'

What could she say? Taryn thought the world of him too. And Mrs Ellington's daughter had been having a terrible time of it. 'Don't worry about a thing,' she replied. 'You've spoken to Mr Compton?'

'He still insists I take as long as I need. But I think he's feeling a bit awkward about asking you to stay on. Apparently he gave you his word that you would leave at the end of this week.'

'I'll go and tell him now that it would suit me better to stay on,' Taryn assured her, and a much relieved permanent housekeeper—who was, after all, a mother first and foremost—went back to looking after her daughter.

'You're sure?' Osgood Compton asked when she told him, his lovely beaming smile surfacing for all he tried to hold it down.

On Saturday, well aware by then that her employer liked to have a nap at some time during the afternoon, Taryn wondered if he might like to sit outside and have his tea. She had made his favourite cake only that morning.

She was in the act of taking a tray of china out to the garden table when the sound of a car coming up the drive drew her attention. So far as she knew Mr Compton was not expecting visitors. That was not to say, however, that his visitors would not be welcome.

Though as she watched the long sleek, this year's model car halt outside the main entrance door, Taryn left what she was doing and hurried outside to it, her protective instincts to the fore. There was only one visitor, she saw, but if this person had accidentally called at the wrong address then she did not want him or her disturbing Mr Compton's nap by ringing the doorbell.

She arrived at the driver's door just as a tall, dark-haired man, somewhere in his mid-thirties, was getting out. He saw her and stiffened—absolutely thunderstruck.

Taryn stared at him. 'Who…?' she began, seeing no reason at all why this man should be staring at her every bit as if he knew her from somewhere.

'What the blazes are *you* doing here?' he demanded, to her utter astonishment.

His attitude had rattled her. 'Do I know you?' she snapped hostilely. But straight on the heels of that came a spark of recognition. He was dressed in shirt and trousers now, which was perhaps why it had taken a minute or two to sink in. But she *had* seen him before, and that time, about two months ago now, he had been immaculately suited and had been carrying an expensive-looking briefcase.

She *did* know him. Shock washed over her. If she was not very much mistaken he was the man who had been in the lift that day she had reeled out of Brian Mellor's office! This man was, in fact, the man she had that day been rude to!

He had demanded to know what the blazes she was doing there. But what on earth was *he* doing here? Taryn thought it was time she found out!

# CHAPTER TWO

WHERE it had taken up to a minute for Taryn to recognise the man, and to recall where she had seen him before, he, it seemed, with barely a glance to her face, blonde hair and trim figure, had at once recognised her. Even though she too had been business-clad at that time.

With his, 'What the blazes are you doing here?' still ringing in the air, she felt at a distinct disadvantage. It was more than time she asked him the same question. 'We aren't expecting visitors,' she told him pointedly.

'Aren't we?' he rapped, clearly not liking the fact that she had taken upon herself the role of the occupant's Rottweiler. And, not deigning to wait for her reply, he, without more ado, strode past her, making for the door she had just come from.

Taryn chased after him. 'Who are you?' she challenged his back.

She thought he was going to ignore her, but he halted and turned about. 'Do I take it that you're the incomparable Taryn the phone lines between here and New York are full of?'

Her eyes widened in amazement. 'You know—?' She broke off. Osgood Compton's daughter lived in New York. 'You have the advantage,' she said, getting her breath back.

'Jake Nash,' he supplied. 'You're my great uncle's temporary, looking-to-be-permanent housekeeper?' he questioned toughly.

'I intend to leave as soon as Mrs Ellington is able to come and take over,' Taryn replied crisply. And as this Jake Nash, somehow happening to be the antagonistic great-nephew of a true gentleman, again made for the door, 'Mr Compton will be having a nap,' she stated quickly, adding reluctantly, 'If you'd like to come with me to the kitchen I'll make you a cup of tea.'

He seemed to hesitate, as if about to demand who did she think she was, to be giving orders to a member of her employer's family. But he stood back after a moment to allow her to go in first. 'That might be a good idea,' he conceded.

He seemed to know his way to the kitchen, but no sooner were they there than she was realising why he had thought it might be a good idea. For in no time, ignoring her suggestion that he take a seat at the kitchen table while she set the kettle to boil, Jake Nash, standing and leaning his tall length against one of the kitchen units, was in there straight away, with one question after another.

'You *are* my uncle's housekeeper?' was the first of many.

'Temporary—and ready to go as soon as his permanent housekeeper's daughter is well enough to be left, and her mother returns,' Taryn answered.

'That's a definite?'

'What does it have to do with you?' she asked snappily, starting to feel more than a touch niggled at his sauce, and giving up all pretence of making this man a pot of tea. 'You're not my employer,' she stated, when she could see from the raised eyebrows that he was a man who just wasn't used to being answered back.

'It seems you've been making yourself more than useful in the short time you've been here?' he said curtly.

'It's what I'm employed to do!'

'To the extent of going on long walks with your employer?'

'Not so very long.'

'To the extent of taking him to the pub?'

'He took me!' she exclaimed, unsure how she suddenly came to be defending herself. 'Excepting for once, when it was pouring with rain and he was getting a little fed up being stuck indoors. Anyway—'

'From what I hear, you've even introduced him to the iniquities of playing darts?' he cut in.

Taryn almost laughed at that. In fact, had she not known better, she would have said that there was a twinkle of laughter in Jake Nash's eyes. But she didn't believe that for a second. 'Just what is this—?' she began. But suddenly, and with shock, what he had said about the phone lines between here and New York being full of her began to take on a startling meaning. 'His daughter—Beryl—she's been in touch with you, hasn't she?'

Jake Nash studied her, and seemed, she thought for one absurd moment, to be a little taken with her dainty features and dark blue eyes. 'She rang my mother,' he agreed.

'She wanted you to come and check me out?' Taryn couldn't quite believe what her intelligence had brought her.

'It's Taryn this, Taryn that. Can you blame her?'

'She thinks I'm after his money!' Taryn exclaimed, aghast. 'That—that he's somehow sm-smitten with me!' Appalled, she could hardly get the words out.

'Beryl has met Mrs Ellington,' he responded evenly. 'She has never met you. You can't blame her for having a daughter's natural concern.'

'So the minute she rang, you hared down here to make sure I—'

'I had business this way today,' he cut in. 'It was no problem to make a detour.

'Jake!' A glad cry from the doorway rent the air. Taryn looked over to where her refreshed temporary employer had just come in, and was grateful in this instance that he was slightly hard of hearing. 'How good to see you!' he exclaimed, as the two men met in the middle of the kitchen and shook hands. She did not want him upset by the unpleasantness of Beryl keeping her eye on her. 'You've obviously introduced yourself to Taryn,' he went on beaming. 'I just can't believe that I've been so lucky with not one housekeeper but two.'

'Would you like tea now?' Taryn asked, feeling Jake Nash's eyes on her, but deciding to ignore him.

'Shall we have it out in the garden?' Osgood Compton asked.

'Perhaps you'd like to carry this tray out?' she addressed Jake pleasantly without looking at him, not seeing why he shouldn't make himself useful. Picking up the tray she had laid earlier, she took it to him, and was glad to have the kitchen to herself when, Mr Compton chatting away, they departed.

Taryn busied herself making a pot of tea, and as she did so began to see that perhaps, in all fairness, Beryl-nee-Compton— she had no idea what her last name was—was only acting as any daughter worthy of the name should. What with her father by the sound of it singing the praises of his temporary housekeeper with every phone call, perhaps it *wasn't* so surprising she should want to know that he wasn't, as it were, being taken for a ride—offensive to her father though that might be.

'You've forgotten the extra cup,' Mr Compton reminded her when she carried a tray of tea and extra hot water out to them.

That he intended she should join them was kind, and had his great-nephew not been there she would have been pleased to have kept him company. But his nephew *was* there and, while she didn't give a button that he might report back on how the housekeeper had joined them for tea, she thought Osgood Compton might enjoy some male company for a change.

'I've got something in the oven I want to keep my eye on,' she stated, though the casserole in the oven she was making ready for the freezer was able to cook quite well on its own, without her watching it.

'If you're sure?' he answered, and then, as she paused a moment to check cake, cake knives, napkins, and that they had everything they would need, 'Taryn's normally in engineering too,' he informed his nephew. 'It was my good fortune that she wanted a break from it when Mrs Ellington had to go...'

'You're an engineer?' Jake Nash asked, every bit as if he was interested.

This time she could not avoid meeting his grey eyes. 'PA,' she replied briefly, and left it at that.

She was on her way back across the lawn when she heard Osgood Compton informing his great-nephew, 'Taryn was a PA at Mellor Engineering. You know them, of course?'

He would know from that too, Taryn realised as she sipped her own tea, why she had been in the building that day. It would not explain, though, why she had given him such short shrift in the lift when he had seen that she was upset. But, from his uncle's comment just now that she had wanted a break from her more normal line of work, it was something of a whopping clue to anyone with a degree of intelligence that the reason she had been upset was because her employment had just been terminated.

It was fairly obvious to her that Jake Nash had much more than a degree of intelligence, but she cared not that he might think she had been dismissed from her post. And she saw no reason whatsoever to tell him that, when it came to terminating her employment, she had been the one to do it.

Taryn all at once realised that she was feeling quite anti. Quite worked up. Quite, quite... Words failed her. She did not like the man. Life here with Mr Compton had been tranquil. This man—Jake Nash—had strode in and shattered that tranquillity—and she did not like that either.

She made herself scarce when from the window she saw that her temporary employer and his nephew, carrying the heaviest tray, were heading for the kitchen. In her view he was Mr Compton's visitor. There was no need at all for the housekeeper to be there to bid him farewell. She escaped to her room.

She left it a few minutes after she had seen his car go down the drive before she went down the stairs again, and was in the kitchen scraping new potatoes for the evening meal when Osgood Compton came looking for her.

'Jake's gone,' he announced needlessly.

'It must have been nice to see him,' she replied. No need for the dear man to know that she knew the true reason for his visit—or for him to know how antagonistic she felt towards the man.

'It was. Especially when he's always so busy,' Osgood agreed.

'He mentioned he had business this way,' Taryn commented non-committally.

'Jake always has business somewhere,' he answered proudly. And added, with yet more pride, 'He heads the Nash Corporation. I expect you've heard of them?'

Taryn stared at him in amazement. Everybody who knew anything about engineering had heard of the Nash Corporation. Not that they dealt only in engineering. They were well known in the design, development and manufacturing world—a corporation that was involved in electronics, engineering and aviation, to name but a few. And Jake Nash headed that corporation!

'I didn't know he was *that* Nash,' she answered with a smile. It did not make her like Jake Nash any better, but his uncle need not know that she was a touch anti-nephew just then.

'He's done well,' he commented—a modest understatement, she felt. Mellor Engineering was quite a large outfit, but it was just not in the same league as the Nash Corporation. 'Jake liked your cake, by the way.'

'Oh, did he?' she replied sunnily.

'He said that if you're half as good a PA as you are a cook, you'll be snapped up the moment you put yourself back on the PA market.'

Too kind! She changed the subject. 'I thought we'd have a chicken salad for dinner.'

'Are you going to make some of that special potato salad you made the other day?' he asked appreciatively. He was a joy to spoil.

Over the next few days Taryn felt her equilibrium start to settle down again. She had wanted that tranquillity back, and by about Wednesday morning she reckoned she had found it. It was not to last.

For all she took care of all the chores, Osgood Compton treated her more like a house guest than a housekeeper. They had enjoyed a shared lunch and, having left him to take what he called 'a little zizz'—his usual afternoon nap—she was in the kitchen preparing vegetables for the evening meal when, to her astonishment, the kitchen door opened and none other than Jake Nash walked in!

Feeling fairly staggered, she asked, 'Where did you leave your car?' craning to see the whole semi-circle of the drive. Where had he sprung from? She rinsed her hands and grabbed up a towel and, turning to face him, began drying them.

'I've walked up from the road. I didn't want to disturb my uncle.'

Didn't want…? Was she to take it from that that he did not want to disturb his uncle's nap—or did she gather that Jake Nash was there to see her? Familiar feelings of hostility butted away tranquillity. 'Come to check I haven't run off with the family silver?' she bridled, dark blue eyes flashing violet sparks.

For answer he gave her a smile of such sinking charm that she almost forgot that she didn't like him. 'We got off on the wrong foot,' he suggested pleasantly, and held out his right hand.

Taryn stared at him, refusing to shake hands. 'You want something?' she said warily.

'We both do,' he acknowledged, his hand dropping back to his side.

'We—do?' She was cagey still.

'Are you going to make me a cup of tea?' he requested.

Taryn turned away to set the kettle to boil, knowing without having to ask that he had not been referring to a cup of tea when he had said he wanted something.

'You'll join me, I hope?' he invited, when he observed she had taken out only one cup and saucer.

No need to be antagonistic just for the sake of it, she decided, taking out another cup and saucer and, since he was not yet ready to go and see his uncle, inviting him to take a seat at the kitchen table.

'Cake?' she offered.

'You heard?'

Her lips twitched. He knew his uncle had passed on his compliment about her cake. She glanced at Jake Nash and saw he had his eyes on her nearly smiling mouth, perhaps noting he had reached her sense of humour. She sobered straight away, and busied herself taking two cups of tea over to the table. Against her sudden better judgement, she took him a slice of cake too.

Since he had invited her to join him, she sat down at the table with him, this good-looking, steady grey-eyed man. 'So,' she challenged, 'if the phone lines from New York haven't been buzzing again, what do you want that I might possibly want too? Presumably you believe there's some sort of connection?'

'You have a sharp intelligence, Taryn,' he commented.

She fixed her dark blue glance on him. 'So I can make a decent cake and I'm not too dim. So?'

'You'll be leaving here soon?'

'Mrs Ellington phoned to say she will definitely be back by the end of next week.'

'When you'll be looking for a job?'

Taryn collapsed back in her chair. 'You're never offering me the job of your housekeeper!' she exclaimed, bringing out that which her 'sharp intelligence' had brought her.

'I'm quite adequately catered for in that department,' he replied smoothly.

'Of course,' she murmured. 'Your good lady will see to all your domestic arrangements.'

'I don't have a "good lady" in that sense.'

'You're not married?'

'Nor living with anyone,' he answered coolly. 'I do have a kind soul who comes in and tidies up and cooks a bit most days.' He shrugged, and challenged, 'You like housekeeping so well that you want to continue with it when your stint for my uncle is done?'

She shook her head. 'I needed a break from PA work—I'm now ready to go back to it.'

'Back to Mellor Engineering?'

Subtle question. 'No,' she replied coldly. 'And, to answer your next question, no, I was not dismissed on the spot,' she informed him defensively.

He eyed her silently for long interminable seconds—and she was sure she was not going to say another word to the wretched man. 'But you did leave—on the spot?' he enquired, with that sharp intelligence *he* had. She refused to answer. 'Care to tell me why?' he persisted.

'No!' she retorted. 'It's nothing to do with you.'

'You—had a small breakdown?' he fished.

'No, I didn't!' she exploded. Honestly, this man! If it was her house she'd chuck him out. She counted to ten, felt calmer and, since he had witnessed for himself that she had been upset that day in the lift, conceded, 'I was—upset—at the time. But now I'm looking for a job I can well and truly get my teeth into.'

'You want a career?' he enquired mildly. But she had a feeling, as steady grey eyes held hers and he took in her every word, look and nuance, that this seemingly mild-at-the-moment man missed not a thing.

'To have a career is paramount to me,' she agreed. 'My first priority.'

'You have a second priority?'

'I could do with finding somewhere to live.'

'Where do you normally live when you're not here in Knights Bromley?'

'At home. In London.'

'With your parents?'

'My parents are divorced.'

'You live with your mother?'

'Honestly!' she gasped. 'Is there no end to your questions?' He smiled, totally unperturbed. And, to her own surprise, she found she was telling him, 'My mother lives in Africa. I live with my father and stepmother, actually.'

'Ah!'

'Ah?' she queried.

'I take it your stepmother is of the wicked variety?'

Her lips twitched again. What was it about this man that even when she was annoyed with him he could make her want to laugh? 'So?' she queried, determined again not to smile.

'So,' he replied, 'while I'll leave you to deal with the second of your problems, I might be able to help with your first.'

Keep up, Taryn, she urged, and realised he must be referring to her first and her second priority. Second was fresh accommodation; first was a PA career job.

She looked at him, seeking more of a clue. He looked back, saying nothing. 'You're saying you have PA vacancies at the Nash Corporation?' she asked, bringing out slowly the only thing she could think he must be meaning.

'From time to time,' he replied, accepting that his great-uncle had told her of his company. 'Though as secretaries are upgraded they are more usually filled internally.'

Taryn was not at all certain that she wanted to work for the Nash Corporation. Even if it was true that, as career moves went, she would be hard put to it to do better. 'But you have one vacancy that you can't fill internally?' she guessed, while at the same time she could hardly credit that Jake Nash, the head of the whole shoot, should be talking to her about it—if indeed this was the case—when it went without saying that he must have a very efficient Human Resources department within his organisation who took care of all that.

He did not answer her question but instead asked her, 'Tell me, Taryn, how long were you working for Mellor Engineering?'

He was interviewing her for a job! She stared at him wide-eyed, and not a little disbelieving. But she saw no harm in answering. 'Five years.'

'Has it been your only job?' he wanted to know.

Apart from her waitressing stint, she had on rare occasions typed out a report or something or other for her aunt or one of her aunt's clients. But Taryn hardly thought he would be interested in that. 'I did an extensive business and secretarial course until I was eighteen, and from there went straight to Mellor Engineering.'

'You were a PA there?'

'Not straight away. I had all the theory I could possibly want. But after three years' actual work in that field, I was promoted to PA to Brian Mellor.' She experienced a moment of surprise that Brian's name had left her lips without the slightest falter.

But there was no time for her to wonder about that, because Jake Nash was going on, 'You worked for Brian Mellor himself? Impressive. You must be good.'

It seemed immodest to retort, I *am*, but Taryn had had enough. 'Look here,' she erupted—a touch arrogantly, it had to be said. 'If you're interviewing me, and I can't see what else this is about, then— while I'm not sure I'm applying for the job anyway—I wouldn't mind hearing what this job actually is. Or even if there *is* a job.'

He did not care for her uppity tone. She could tell that from the slight narrowing of his eyes. But, whatever he was thinking or feeling, he covered it well to inform her, 'There is a job...'

'A PA's job?' She might be interested, she might not be. But, since this was her career she was thinking of, it had to be PA or nothing.

'Yes,' he agreed, but warned, 'It may only be temporary.'

'I'm not interested in temporary,' she said straight away. 'I'm not even sure I'm interested anyway.'

'Of course you are!' he countered bluntly, causing her to think he needed a slap.

'Why "of course"?' Her tone was belligerent—she'd never had a job interview like it!

'The experience you'd gain alone would stand you in very good stead when you're ready to move on. As my PA you'd—'

'*Your* PA!' she gasped. Oh, no, not on your life! But her head was instantly abuzz. They didn't come any higher than Jake Nash—and he was suggesting she might be his PA!

'The vacancy isn't common knowledge yet,' he replied.

'You're getting rid of your present PA?' Taryn exclaimed, her dark blue eyes saucer-wide.

'I wouldn't dream of it; she's far too valuable.'

'I've lost you somewhere,' Taryn owned, feeling in quite a fog.

He took pity on her. 'Kate Lambert has worked for me for the last seven years. I confess I'd be totally lost without her.'

'But you're thinking of letting her go—temporarily?' Taryn had stayed with him so far.

He threw some light into her darkness. 'Kate, in confidence, is newly pregnant.'

'Ah!' Taryn breathed. 'You want maternity cover for her?'

'A bit more than that. To put it mildly, Kate is having a pretty torrid time of it. And while in normal times she copes excellently with what I appreciate is a very exacting job, her pregnancy seems to be taking a lot out of her. Poor Kate—she is quite drained at times.'

'She is easily tired?' Taryn put in.

'I'm afraid so. And while, in order to have longer with the baby when it arrives, she wants to carry on working as long as she possibly can, I think she is already finding it quite a struggle.'

By the sound of it he wasn't thinking of taking on someone for cover only while Kate Lambert was away, but someone sooner. 'It's temporary, this job?' Taryn questioned.

'Kate says she wants to return at the end of her maternity leave. I'd be more than pleased if she does.'

'But you don't think she will come back?'

'Kate's a perfectionist. She'll want to do both jobs, being a mother and being a PA, in perfect fashion. I think there's every chance she'll want to stay home if she can.'

That seemed natural enough to Taryn. But she was suddenly startled to realise she was starting to be interested—even to the extent that she might end up working for this man she did not like. No, she denied, she definitely did not want to work for him. Hang on a minute, though. As he had suggested, any experience she gained while working for him would be invaluable and, as he'd said, would stand her in very good stead when she went on to her next job. 'How soon would you want me to start?' she asked.

'Not so fast, Taryn,' he replied. 'I haven't offered you the job.'

She flushed red, and had never felt more embarrassed. 'Forgive me,' she said coolly. 'I thought you had—were…'

'I'm sorry,' he apologised, his eyes on her flushed skin. He smiled gently. 'I'm not used to this initial interview practice.' And, having taken the blame on himself, 'Human Resources would normally deal with that, but I don't intend to involve them at the moment. Nor have I told Kate yet that I'm looking for someone to work in tandem with her who would carry on to cover her while she's on maternity leave,' he said, going on to explain, 'Kate's hopes have been dashed too often in the past, apparently, and she had started to believe she would never have a baby. Because she is having such a tough time—yet still fearful something might go wrong—she has asked me to not tell anyone of her condition.'

'She doesn't know you're getting someone to take some of her workload?' Taryn asked, as that bit jumped out at her. 'Will she mind?'

'Hopefully, when she adjusts to the idea, she'll be all for it. My thoughts were—seeing that you want to get back into PA work—

that I'd see how you felt about coming to work for me, then ask you to come into the office at your first opportunity. Kate can then tell you what the job entails, and she can also judge if she thinks you're capable of doing it.'

'And you will have the final yea or nay?'

He nodded. 'That's right,' he acknowledged. 'I know I've rather dropped this on you,' he added. 'I'll ring you early next week, when you've had chance to consider how you feel.'

With that he got to his feet, just as his great uncle came into the kitchen. 'Jake!' he said gladly. 'I didn't see or hear your car!'

'I needed to stretch my legs,' Jake replied easily. 'I walked up from the road.'

Taryn got up and refilled the kettle, knowing her present temporary employer would like some tea. But as he smiled at her, and he and his great-nephew ambled out to look at some machine part Osgood Compton had unearthed and they had been discussing last Saturday, she could not help but still feel stunned that it looked as if she might possibly have a new temporary employer within the same family! Did she want to work for Jake Nash, though?

It was a question that would return again and again to plague her over the next few days. But even as the weekend came and went she was still unsure—always supposing the job was offered.

She did not like him. Against that, though, did she *have* to like him? She had loved her previous employer and ultimately, because of that love, she'd had to leave that job.

By no chance would that happen if she did go to work for Jake Nash. Theirs would be a strictly professional working relationship. Love certainly wouldn't come into it. No, basically, she did not have to like him.

Mrs Ellington telephoned on Monday and said she would be returning on Thursday morning. And, knowing then that she would be leaving on Thursday afternoon, Taryn acknowledged that, as sweet and lovely as Osgood Compton was, she had had sufficient of keeping house.

What she wanted was a job she could knuckle down to. A career job. One that would take her to the top of the PA tree. She had to smile at that—the top did not come any higher than PA to Jake Nash, albeit temporary, albeit in tandem with his invaluable and present PA.

He, Jake Nash, had left her to consider how she felt. He had told her it was a temporary job and that she would only be assisting Kate Lambert until she went off to have her baby. But when Taryn put her mind to considering the experience she would gain, she knew by Tuesday morning that she wanted the job.

The problem was, would she get it? From what she could remember she had rarely shown Jake Nash anything other than her antagonistic side. And while it was true, as he said, that they had started off 'on the wrong foot', it was odd that should be so. She was usually much more amiable with people she came into contact with. Which led her to wonder, given that she had been slightly off with him from the word go, would he *want* her working with him?

On pondering over it, as she pottered about making everything spick and span so that Mrs Ellington would not have to roll her sleeves up and get into heavy work as soon as she returned, Taryn realised that, while she did not like Jake Nash, he would see no need for him to have to like her either. All he would require from whoever he took on would be someone he could confidently leave to keep his office running smoothly. Someone who would work hard and not put down her pen at the stroke of five.

Well, she could do that, and she never had been a clock-watcher.

Though before she got chance to prove that, there were hurdles to clear. It was plain now why he had not put this temporary vacancy through his Human Resources section. With Kate Lambert not wanting it broadcast that she was pregnant, he had decided that he personally would deal with the issue of getting her some help.

Briefly Taryn wondered why he had not thought of sounding out someone within the company to assist Kate Lambert. But that did not take too much thinking about. Kate's assistant had to be someone with PA experience. And any experienced PA within the group would already be assigned to someone in management. And, while perhaps they would be happy for the chance to work for the head of the corporation, they might not feel so happy when Kate Lambert's maternity leave expired and—despite what Jake Nash had said about Kate maybe deciding to stay home with her baby—she wanted to come back and take over again.

But, putting first things first, by the time she was serving dinner that night Taryn had begun to feel quite edgy that Jake Nash had not yet fulfilled his promised to ring her 'early next week'. If he didn't ring her soon she wouldn't be there for him *to* ring!

Which, with her feeling all on edge, perhaps explained why she was not at her most friendly when the phone rang that evening. Dinner was over and Osgood Compton, having earlier spoken with his daughter and not expecting another call, was in his garage, inspecting his beloved Daimler Double Six car.

'Hello?' Taryn queried, picking up the phone and admitting to churning insides.

'Jake Nash,' answered a well-remembered voice, to set her antagonistic vibes a-flutter—what *was* it about this man? 'You've had time to consider our discussion?' he enquired, getting straight down to business, apparently only needing to hear her say that one word 'hello' to know he had got the right person.

Although logically, Taryn supposed, since she was the only female supposed to be there, it would not take an awful lot of guesswork. 'I'd like to come and see Kate Lambert,' she replied. Two could play the straight-down-to-business game.

He didn't say *good*, but, since neither did he say that he had reconsidered, Taryn took it that, subject to her passing muster with his present PA, she was still in there with a chance. 'Has my uncle's housekeeper advised when she's returning?'

'Thursday morning,' Taryn replied. And before she could draw another breath began to understand that Jake Nash had no time to waste.

'Kate will see you at eleven-thirty Friday,' he decided—and, take it or leave it, he was gone.

For all of ten seconds, feeling more than a touch put out, Taryn felt like telling him what she could do with his decisiveness. But when she had calmed down she knew that she still very much wanted that job.

Mrs Ellington arrived as promised on Thursday morning. Taryn prepared lunch for both Mrs Ellington and Osgood Compton, and was then happy to relinquish the reins of what had after all only been meant to be a two-week fill-in job. She bade an affectionate farewell to Osgood Compton, and left his tranquil home.

That her own home was far from tranquil was an abrupt reminder to Taryn that she needed to find somewhere else to live.

'Thank goodness you're back,' her stepmother greeted her. From that Taryn knew that the new housekeeper had not stayed the course.

'What would you like for dinner?' she asked. She might as well volunteer to cook it as wait to be asked; she knew she would be doing the honours anyway.

Her family's domestic arrangements were far from her mind the next morning, however. She dressed with care in a fine wool navy suit, the skirt's length just touching her knees. She wanted to look her best, and was glad she had good legs. They were long, shapely, and she was blessed with trim ankles to go with them.

Taryn owned to butterflies in her tummy as she drove to the offices of the Nash Corporation. She wanted this job, and hoped she would be lucky enough to get it. She reminded herself that she knew PA work, was a speedy typist, had good computer skills and—most important—had been told she had an efficient but natural and warm way of dealing with people.

She left her car hoping that Kate Lambert would like her, and that she would assess her as being up to the job. Only then, Taryn knew, would she get through to be interviewed for real by Jake Nash himself. The final decision would rest with him.

Taryn took to Kate Lambert on sight. Kate was short, dark-haired and somewhere past thirty. 'Come in,' she greeted her warmly, shaking her hand as the security man who had shown Taryn up to the top floor went away. 'Would you like coffee?' she asked.

'Please,' Taryn answered with a smile, thinking that it would set a friendly tone, but wanting to make it herself—Kate Lambert looked more than a shade delicate.

'Jake—Mr Nash—he explained the—um—confidential circumstances of the vacancy?' Kate began.

It was a fact that in a few months or so the PA would not be able to hide that she was going to have a baby, but for now Taryn would not have been able to tell. 'Yes, he did. Congratulations,' she replied, wanting to say more, but not wanting to appear gushing.

Kate smiled her thanks, and then got down to asking Taryn about her work to date, and to letting her know some of what was involved in being a PA to a high-powered executive. And the more she spoke, the more she whetted Taryn's appetite for the job. She would ultimately, while Kate was on maternity leave, be running the office of the top executive. She would be dealing with people from all over the world and would be in attendance at 'top brass' meetings. The job was no sinecure, and it paid extraordinarily well. But Taryn was under no illusions; from what Kate was saying, she would earn every penny of the fantastic salary.

It would be a wonderful challenge, Taryn felt, experiencing a buzz in her very bones. She had known before she had come to the Nash Corporation building today that she wanted the job. But the more Kate explained the work she would be doing, the more eager Taryn felt to take it on.

'How do you feel?' Kate asked. 'Have I put you off?'

'Not at all!' Taryn exclaimed enthusiastically. 'It sounds very much the kind of work I would love to be involved with.'

'You're aware the job will only last a year tops?'

Taryn agreed that she was. 'Just until you return from having your baby.'

'Good,' Kate commented. And, causing Taryn's hopes that Kate was ready to recommend her to rise, 'I wouldn't be at all surprised if we didn't find a way of keeping you on in one of the other offices in a year's time.' Then, confirming Taryn's hopes, 'I'll just check if Mr Nash is free to see you now.'

From that Taryn realised that, had Kate Lambert thought her unsuitable, she would have said something to the effect that they would write to her, and would then have bidden her goodbye. But the fact that Kate was phoning through to ask Jake Nash if he was free indicated to Taryn that things had gone well. What she had to do now was hope that her interview with Jake Nash went equally well.

'Mr Nash says to give him five minutes,' Kate reported, coming off the phone. 'Now, is there anything you would like to ask me?'

To Taryn's mind they had discussed everything pretty thoroughly. And just then Kate had to take a call, so Taryn was left starting to feel the nip of nerves. Very shortly she would be seeing a man who always before had seemed to bring out the worst in her. Only today, if she was to have any chance of this job she was now realising she wanted so badly, she must hold down those impulses to spark up at him.

It was most unfortunate in her view that, when she had worked for a whole two years for Brain Mellor without once feeling the need to fire up at him, Jake Nash had barely to say more than a few sentences and she was straight in there. But there was no comparing the two—one ex-employer and one new one, hopefully.

Brian for the main part had been placid and easygoing. Jake Nash just had the knack…

The door opened. And there, business-suited, tall, dark-haired and just as she remembered him, stood Jake Nash. 'Sorry to have kept you,' he offered urbanely. 'Come in, Taryn.'

Taryn got to her feet, her heart giving a funny little skip. She preceded him into his office—a large, light and airy affair, with a couple of other doors leading from it, one to the outside corridor, she guessed, the other probably a cloakroom of some sort.

There was a three-piece suite—a three-seater sofa and two matching armchairs—at the far end of the room. But it was to an upright chair by the side of his desk that Jake Nash indicated when he invited, 'Take a seat.' As she did so, he went round to his chair behind the desk. 'Kate has filled you in on what is expected?' he enquired.

'It all sounds very interesting,' Taryn agreed. Actually, he had rather nice eyes—and, her eyes strayed, his mouth wasn't all that bad either. Good heavens! Taryn brought herself up short—what on earth was she thinking of?

'And how do you feel about it?'

She started to feel scratchy with him again. The very fact that she was still there should have told him that she was interested. 'I believe I can do the work,' she replied.

He took that in, and enquired bluntly, 'You appreciate that some of the work in this office is highly confidential?'

'Confidentiality, is all part of a PA's remit in my view,' she replied.

Jake Nash did not appear too impressed—she would have given anything to know what went on behind that cool exterior. 'You'll be able to supply references, of course?'

'I…' She hesitated.

'You seem unsure?' He was straight in, and again Taryn felt her antagonism fairy give her a poke.

'It isn't…' she began. Somehow she felt awkward about Brian

Mellor being approached for a reference, even though she did not doubt he would give her a good one. 'I've only ever had the one permanent employer,' she stated, as calmly as she could in the circumstances.

'And you left him in rather a hurry,' Jake Nash said, not a smile or anything the least encouraging about him. 'Why was that?' he demanded sharply.

With difficulty Taryn reined in the spurt of aggravation his sharp tone aroused. He wanted confidentiality, she'd give him confidential! 'That's confidential,' she stated, making no apology.

'I'll accept confidentiality in business,' her would-be employer retorted. 'But your reason for leaving was personal.'

'How do you make that out?' she flared.

'That it was personal? I'd have thought that was obvious!' he rapped, and was unrelenting when he demanded, 'Why did you and Brian Mellor fall out?'

'We didn't fall out!' she denied, aware that this job she had coveted was getting away from her, but feeling powerless to do anything to stop it.

'Oh, come on,' Jake Nash grated impatiently. 'You stayed with the man for two whole years and then walked out at a moment's notice? According to you, Brian Mellor didn't dismiss you—so it had to be personal.'

'He didn't dismiss me!' she said forcefully, twin spots of angry colour appearing in her cheeks.

'So why leave without first giving him the courtesy of at least a month's warning that you were resigning?'

He had a point, she supposed. From his point of view he would not want her trained in the smooth running of his office only for her to up and leave on the spot over some whim of the moment.

He was still waiting for an answer, she could tell that, but no way was she going to tell him that Brian Mellor had kissed her. Not only did that seem to her to be disloyal to Brian, and to his marriage, but in this day and age this sophisticated man with his now icy grey eyes concentrated on her would probably laugh his socks off.

'If you must know…' she began, floundering—and all at once she'd had it with this man. It was touch and go whether she still had a chance of this job anyway. She decided to give him the truth and to the devil with him. 'If you must know,' she said again, heatedly this time, 'I fell in love with him!' There—it was out. She was blushing furiously, but there—pick the bones out of that.

'Oh, my…' Jake Nash leant back in his chair. 'His wife didn't care for it?'

'His wife didn't know.' Honestly! This man! 'Neither did he,' she charged on, before he could ask—which she full well knew he would.

Jake Nash surveyed her for long unspeaking seconds. Then casually, while still surveying her, 'I'm damned sure that there's more to it than that,' he drawled. 'Tell me, Miss Webster, do you make a habit of falling in love with every man who employs you?'

And that did it! Sarcastic pig! He had obviously noted the affection she felt for his great-uncle. And now this—her owning up to loving the employer before him. Taryn got to her feet. She knew then without a shadow of a doubt that she had not got the job. 'Every time,' she answered, as he too got to his feet. 'Though in your case it would have been extremely easy to make an exception!'

As an exit line, she felt it was rather good. But before she could take so much as one step towards the door Jake Nash, to her utter amazement, burst out laughing. It was so unexpected that she just stood there and stared at him—stared at his firm mouth, now uplifted at the corners, his white even teeth revealed.

'Oh, Taryn Webster,' he said, shaking his head. 'Let us be thankful for small mercies.' And while she was still standing there, staring at him, his right hand suddenly shot out. 'Be here at nine o'clock sharp on Monday,' he instructed.

Taryn was so stunned her own right hand came out, and this time, having once before refused to do so, she did shake hands with him, the warmth of his skin as his larger hand covered her dainty one giving her something of a tingle.

'You're saying—I've got the job?' she asked, hardly believing her cross-tempered interview was ending like this.

'You've got the job,' he confirmed. 'Let's hope neither of us lives to regret it.'

# CHAPTER THREE

TARYN had been working for Jake Nash for a month when it suddenly struck her that she had not thought of Brian Mellor in a long, long while. She found that realisation more than a little startling. But more startling still was the unbelievable truth that not once in the month she had been working for Jake had she wished that she was back working for Brian! Taryn almost gasped out loud in shock when, following on from that she had to consider—did she still love Brian?

It came as a bolt from the blue when a second or two later she recognised that—neither missing working for him and seeing him daily, nor even so much as thinking of him recently—love him she did not.

Two years and more she had spent loving him. Yet in the space of a few months she was on the way to forgetting him completely. Not that there was time to think about anything but work when she was in the office. But...

She was on her way there now, and had space that morning to dwell on something other than helping Kate run a streamlined unit. Taryn saw then that she had really needed to get out of an office environment for those two months she had worked for Jake's great-uncle. She had needed to take a step back. But, oh, how glad she was to be back in the swing of it.

Working for Jake—he had told her to use his first name after she'd

Mr Nash-ed him a few times—had been a revelation. He was always first into the office—always there before she got there anyway. That was when he wasn't abroad on business, when they wouldn't see him for days. But she instantly knew when he was back—there was always a buzz about the place when Jake was around.

Taryn parked her car and went swinging into the building. Her co-workers no longer strangers, she greeted those she knew and headed for the lifts. On her first day at the Nash Corporation Kate had taken her round the offices she would need to liaise with and introduced her as her assistant. Everyone had been very friendly, and had accepted what Kate had said.

Everyone, that was, with the exception of Dianne Farmer, a tall, well-groomed woman in her mid-twenties, who had said quite sharply, 'I'd have applied for the job, had I known of the vacancy.'

'It's only a temporary position while I work on another assignment,' Kate had placated her. But later she had confided to Taryn that Jake wouldn't have Dianne Farmer working for him at any price.

'She's not up to the work?'

Kate had smiled. 'I think she could possibly do it, but she makes it fairly obvious that she fancies him.'

'Oh,' Taryn murmured. 'He likes to do his own hunting?'

'And how!' Kate agreed. 'But he wouldn't dream of dating anybody who works here anyway. He has no room for that sort of entanglement in his business life.'

Taryn had to smile to herself. She had thought she had blown her chances of this job when she had flared that she'd make an exception and *not* fall in love with him. All too obviously that had been a point in her favour and had clinched the job for her.

It was Kate who had most to do with him, but he would occasionally call Taryn in to take down some dictation. She had been right in her guess about the two other doors in his office, she discovered. One did lead to the outside corridor, the other to a cloakroom.

But it was more than a cloakroom, Taryn had found. Because

Kate was very often queasy, and bearing in mind that she did not want anyone to know of her pregnancy just yet, Jake had kindly suggested she use his facilities if she felt a sudden need to sprint to the staff powder room.

On one such occasion, with Jake elsewhere at the time, Kate had made a dive for his office. When Taryn felt she had been gone long enough, and went looking for her in case she needed help of any sort, she'd found her grey-faced and hanging on to the washbasin.

'Oh, Lord!' Kate exclaimed weakly. 'My Mother never told me it would be like this.'

Taryn guided her into Jake's office. 'Sit down here,' she said gently. 'I'll go and tidy up in there.'

Kate gratefully, if groggily, sat down. She had, Taryn saw, managed to rinse away all evidence of using any of the facilities, which left her little to do but straighten the towel on the rail. As she did so she observed the shower in the room, and the fact that there was a dinner suit hanging on one of the several pegs. Jake was invariably the last to leave. Quite plainly he would be working late that night, and intended to shower and change before going on to some formal sort of function straight from the office.

That he had outside interests that were not formal was plain too. Answering the phone when she had only been working there a few days, Taryn had heard a very sultry voice ask to speak to Mr Nash.

'Just a moment,' Taryn had requested, and, with her hand over the receiver, having previously been advised to enquire first before putting calls throughout, 'Louise Taylor?' she asked Kate.

'That's a new one. You'd better ask him,' Kate advised.

Taryn put her caller on hold and rang through to the next door office. 'I've a Louise Taylor on the line,' she told Jake when he answered.

'Put her through,' he replied. 'Louise!' she heard him welcome her, and sharply cut her own connection.

Yes, she had learned a lot this last month, Taryn reflected as the lift stopped at the top floor and she went along to the office she shared with Kate. It amazed her how much work Kate got through, but Taryn liked to think she was starting to be of some help to her.

For once though, Kate—who struggled valiantly to get to work on time—was not there. 'Good morning, Taryn.' Jake Nash, having heard her, strolled though the open communicating door. She saw his eyes flick over her face and trim shape. She was wearing a black trouser suit over a crisp white shirt. He might draw the line at actually dating one of his employees, but his glance was appreciative on her, Taryn felt. 'Kate's phoned through—she's had a foul weekend. I've told her not to come in today. Do you think you can cope?'

Oh, help! 'No problem,' Taryn replied brightly—and hoped she sounded as if she meant it.

So began a day like none other that she had ever known. The morning sped by. She tackled everything that came her way for what she thought was the first hour—only to discover, when she glanced at her watch while holding on a phone call, that it was a quarter to one. Where had the morning gone?

She took a break from her desk at twenty past one and went along to the staff canteen. She did not have time to stop for a meal, but purchased a sandwich to take back to her desk. She was actually making her way back there when she bumped into Robin Cooper, one of the 'suits' from the top floor, who had previously asked her to go out with him.

'Today I feel lucky,' he said as he fell into step with her.

'That's nice,' she replied.

He sent her his best smile. 'Today I feel as if, should I ask you out, you might well say yes.'

She laughed. 'You're a tryer. I'll give you that.'

'That's a yes, then, is it?'

He was amusing. She was still smiling as she reached her office door. She opened it. 'Perhaps today's not so lucky for you after all.'

'You're heartless, Taryn!' he cried plaintively.

'I know,' she answered solemnly, and went in and closed the door on him.

'Who was that?' asked a voice from the inner sanctum.

She had thought Jake had gone out, but the fact that the communicating door between the two offices was open indicated that he must have come in looking for her.

She followed through her thought. 'Is there something I can help you with?'

'Robin Cooper,' he stated, clearly following through his own thoughts.

'One and the same,' she agreed.

'And you're heartless because you wouldn't go out with him?' he guessed.

My, what big ears we have! 'There are only so many days in the week,' she replied lightly.

'Meaning you've a long line of hopefuls queuing up to date you?'

Since it seemed to her that never a day went by without some female or other ringing to speak to him, Taryn felt she would be letting her side down if she allowed him to think she stayed home nights.

'Some nights I just have to stay in and wash my hair,' she murmured.

She saw his lips twitch, and then saw him frown—every bit as if he did not care much for his second PA having such a busy social life she had to invent washing her hair to get the chance of an evening to herself.

Utter rot, of course. It was nothing to him what she did when she was not at work. And his frown soon disappeared when he stated, 'I intended to have a word with you today about your work.'

Her heart plummeted. She wasn't satisfactory? He was

getting rid of her? Only then, when it looked as if she was in danger of losing this job, did she realise how much she wanted to hang on to it. 'Have I done something wrong?' she asked, hoping her feelings of panic weren't showing. She loved the work she was doing.

'Far from it.' He put her out of her misery straight away. 'Come in and take a seat.' Taryn did as he asked, but when she was seated to the side of his desk she was still unsure.

'That's good,' she commented, her large dark blue eyes fixed on him.

'The thing is,' he began, 'Kate was hoping that as her pregnancy progressed, as her body adjusted, she would begin to feel better. But it's a long time happening.'

'She works hard,' Taryn said quickly. 'Kate—'

'You've no need to jump to her defence,' Jake cut in, his well-shaped mouth quirking upwards. 'I'm fully aware of the efforts Kate makes to pretend she's feeling on top form. But she *isn't* feeling on top form. She's tired, not to say exhausted.' He paused. 'And that is where you come in.'

'You know that I'll do anything I can to help.'

'Good,' he said. 'Tell me—how has today gone, working on your own?'

'I've been busy, as you'd expect,' she replied. Working in over-drive would not have been an understatement.

'But given the fact you haven't had time to have a proper meal,' he commented, eyeing the cellophane packaged sandwich she still held in her hands, 'you've coped?'

'And enjoyed it,' she owned—which she had.

'That pleases me,' he allowed, but went on, 'I've decided I don't want Kate working the hours she does—the extra hours she does. I want her to go home on time. Earlier if she feels the need.' Grey eyes looked into wide blue-violet eyes. 'Is that all right with you?'

'Fine by me,' Taryn replied unhesitatingly. 'But will it be fine with Kate?'

'This baby is vitally important to her. I'm sure she'll see sense. It will mean, though, that a lot of the hard graft will fall on your shoulders.'

'Working late is no problem to me,' Taryn assured him.

Jake Nash looked solemnly at her for long moments, and she wasn't sure there was not a twinkle in his eyes when casually he let fall, 'I should hate to be the one to ruin your social life.'

Solemnly she looked back. 'There's no fear of that,' she answered, and found the greatest difficulty in keeping her lips from twitching.

Back at her desk, she ate her sandwich and thought over the conversation she'd just had with Jake..As she had told him, working late was not a problem to her. In fact, with her home life not that brilliant, she would cheerfully come in to work Saturday and Sunday if need be.

But it was not only that. Recalling her feelings of panic when she had thought he was about to ask her to leave, Taryn realised that it wasn't only the work she enjoyed, but that she absolutely loved working for *him!* Now, wasn't that odd? She had started off not liking the man very much at all, but over this past month she had witnessed his sharp and incisive mind, seen him at work, seen him make impossibly tough decisions, and found she could only admire him. For if she and Kate worked hard, then he was no slacker. He could clear his desk quicker than that, deal with budding crises long before they peaked. In fact, Jake Nash was a giant of a man when it came to business.

Exactly how tired and exhausted Kate felt was proved to Taryn when Kate came out from a 'closed doors' discussion with their employer the next day. She seemed to have accepted his proposal for the new working of his office with very little objection.

'Jake tells me he had a little chat with you,' she began. 'Will you mind very much working all hours, Taryn?'

'Not a bit—if you don't mind. I mean, you'll still be here to advise me most of the time, and the experience I'll gain when I eventually leave will take me on to be a PA anywhere.'

Since with a few exceptions most of the PAs in the building made their way homewards come five o'clock, Kate's flexible hours were not commented upon.

Kate had a doctor's appointment on Friday afternoon and left around three. She would not be coming back that day. It had been a busy day—Taryn was beginning to think that there were not any days that were not—and she was in Jake's office, collecting some letters she had left for his signature, when the phone rang. Even though it would probably be for him, she nipped back to her own office to take the call.

Reaching for her pen and notepad as she sat down, she picked up the phone. 'Mr Nash's office,' she greeted the caller.

'That must be my favourite cousin,' said a dear voice she would know anywhere.

'Matt!' she exclaimed delightedly. He worked for an oil company and had been out of the country for an age.

'The very same. How about dinner tonight? Or has some swine pipped me to the post?'

'You mean *swain*,' she laughed.

'No, I don't,' he denied.

She laughed again. Matt, her aunt Hilary's son, was ten years older than Taryn, and Taryn loved him like a favourite brother. 'I'd love to have dinner with you, Matt,' she answered, and without re-alising where her eyes were focussing looked up and into the next office to find that Jake Nash had stopped what he was doing and was looking at her, positively glowering.

The sauce of it! Not ten minutes since she had put a very breathy Sophie Austin through to him—and here he was, by the look of it objecting to her taking a personal call. Well, could he go and boil his head! While it was true she had quite a lot to do if she was to clear her desk for the weekend, he should know by now that clear her desk she would before she went home—regardless of her social commitments.

'I'll call for you at seven, shall I?' Matt asked.

She'd be damned if she'd hurry her phone call just because *he* was watching! 'That will be lovely. You can come and say hello to my father.'

'That'll probably include the dreaded second Mrs Webster,' Matt said wickedly, and she just had to laugh again.

'See you later,' she said, and just had to tell him, 'Lovely to hear you, Matt.'

'You too, sweetheart,' he replied, and was gone.

Taryn was still feeling a smidgen anti-Jake Nash when she went back into his office. What she did not need was his aggressive jibe of, 'It sounds as if *Matt* has his feet well and truly under your family's table!'

Had he not sounded so aggressive, and had she not been feeling that little bit miffed with one head of the Nash Corporation just then—she had slaved for him all week, and he resented one solitary personal phone call!—she might have said that Matt was her cousin. But Jake *had* been aggressive, and she *was* miffed—so yah-boo! 'He has,' she replied snootily.

He did not like her tone. 'And does your father know Matt is married?' he asked nastily.

Never before had Taryn felt like hitting someone; she came very close to doing so just then. Because, having no way of knowing whether Matt was married or unmarried, what Jake Nash was intimating was that she was not interested in any man unless he *was* married.

Her palm itched, but somehow, feeling hurt *and* miffed, Taryn controlled herself. 'Oh, yes,' she replied, outwardly calm. 'If I'm not mistaken my father has met Matt's wife.'

Feeling choked suddenly, Taryn picked up the letters folder and got out of there. There *was* one swine on her horizon—and she could only thank her lucky stars that he would never be her swain!

Taryn was late leaving the office that night. She was still feeling mightily miffed with Jake Nash, and had she not so loved the work she did she felt she would have been tempted to tell him what he could do with his job. Against doing that, though, was the fact that Kate would have to begin all over again in training up someone in the workings of the office. Also, Jake Nash had stressed at her job interview that he had thought it discourteous that she had left her last job without giving notice. He would just love it if she walked out on him on the spot—not that he'd give a damn about courtesy if he wanted her out, she fumed. Then she had to laugh—she was getting herself all worked up over nothing.

Her stepmother was not too pleased that she was rushing to get ready to go out the moment she got in. But to Taryn the joy of seeing Matt again more than made up for the icy displeasure of the woman her father had married.

'Are you back for long?' her father asked Matt. He was very fond of his sister's child, Matt perhaps being the son he would have liked to have had.

'A month or two,' Matt answered, then chatted a while and promised to come over on Sunday.

'Come to lunch. Bring your mother,' Horace Webster invited, his head so above matters domestic that it would not occur to him to give a thought as to who was going to cook it.

A few minutes later and Matt was saying that they had better go or they would be late for their reservation.

'How's your love-life?' he asked Taryn as they drove along.

'Who's got time for a love-life?'

'Still carrying a torch for Brian Mellor?' he asked quietly.

Shocked, Taryn turned to stare at him. 'How did you know about that?' She hadn't told a soul—well, apart from Jake Nash, and he'd only got that out of her by making her cross.

'Lucky guess, I suppose,' Matt replied. 'Though what with two and two adding up to four, and Mother telling me you'd walked out on him and were adamant you weren't going back, it had to be something to do with him. You were too used to the work you did for him for that to have been the cause of your upset.' Taryn did not answer. And Matt, sensitive to her feelings, gently went on, 'Does it still hurt, love?'

Pride would have her instinctively saying, *Not a bit*. But it was the truth—it did *not* hurt. Not a bit. 'I'm over it,' she said, and, having believed for two whole years that she loved Brian Mellor, was only then staggered to wonder, had it ever *been* love? Had it been love she had felt for him? Or had it just been affection and admiration for a man who was basically a very nice person? 'How about you?' she asked, sensitive in return to her dear cousin, who had been devastated when his marriage had hit the rocks.

'I haven't seen Alison since I returned,' he replied. 'I want her back, but these months apart have made me realise that I was doing myself no favours by camping out on her doorstep.' Taryn touched his hand, finding his hurt hard to take. 'But more fish in the sea—or something equally trite,' he said brightly. 'You still going around with your group of chums?'

'Not so much these days,' she answered, having seen little of the gang she had known for years who, just lately, she felt she had grown a little away from.

It was good to be out with her cousin. They had always been able to talk about pretty much anything. But as he drove her home after their meal Taryn realised that, although they had talking the hours away, she had little recollection of anything in particular they had spoken of.

'I won't come in,' Matt said, dropping her off at her home. 'But I'll try and look forward to the family lunch on Sunday.'

He made her laugh, and she went indoors smiling to find her

stepmother—after spending such a pleasurable time with Matt—especially acid and difficult to take.

She must make more of an effort to find somewhere else to live, Taryn decided. Her working days were too full for her to have time to remember to phone a letting agent, much less visit one—always supposing she could find time to look at anything they might have on their books. She made up her mind she would make some phone calls tomorrow.

Only the next day seemed to be spent in shopping for Sunday's meal, tidying, cleaning and dusting, to make the house presentable for their luncheon guests.

Taryn greeted her aunt warmly on Sunday, as always pleased to see her, absently noting that she was toting a briefcase, and not missing the cool exchange between Hilary and her step-mother.

'Eva.' Her aunt acknowledged the lady who to all intents and purposes was her hostess.

'Hilary,' the other responded coolly.

Matt was just his loveable self and seemed above it all, complimenting his step-aunt on the meal—and she graciously accepted his compliments, for all she hadn't so much as peeled a potato towards it.

She went to rest after coffee was served, and Matt went with his uncle to see what things new and spectacular were being cooked up by Horace Webster in his workshop.

'Taryn,' Hilary Kiteley began slowly, once they were alone. 'I need your help.'

Taryn had an idea that she knew what was coming. 'I wondered why you'd brought your briefcase,' she remarked lightly.

'Am I so very obvious?' She did not wait for an answer, but quickly disclosed, 'I've been very badly let down,' and went on to explain how one of her very highest top-notch clients had entrusted her with a most in-depth and complicated report he required typing, and which she had assured him would be not the smallest problem. 'But then Ella, my best girl, caught a virus and couldn't do it—she's still off—and so I gave it to someone else, and—well, to be honest, she has made a total dog's breakfast of it.'

'I'd love to type it for you,' Taryn volunteered, to save her aunt any more awkwardness she might feel at having to ask.

'Would you?' Hilary beamed. 'Oh, you don't know what a relief that is! The silly girl wiped it from her computer without saving it, so although you'll have her typescript, you'll need to type straight from his handwriting so as not to follow her mistakes.'

'No problem,' Taryn promised. 'When does he want it?' she asked, thinking that if she tackled the report, say, for an hour or so every evening—depending how late she was working at the Nash Corporation—she should have it well on the way to completion by Wednesday.

'Er…' Her aunt's hesitation forewarned her of a bit of a snag to the plan. 'I've—um—promised him it will be ready for collection as soon as I have my office open tomorrow,' she confessed.

'You want it for nine tomorrow morning?' Taryn asked, wondering if she would get to see her bed at all that night, and half wishing she had not so readily volunteered.

'You hate me, right?'

In actual fact, though Taryn would have liked to start work on the report straight away, she could not go to the study until their guests had left. She was further held up when her father invited them to stay to tea. Then some friends of his whom he hadn't seen in an age stopped by, and it all started to get away from her.

Although she was eager to take a look at the report, she knew that her stepmother would never let her hear the last of it if she didn't clear up the kitchen after Horace Webster's friends—who had little to do with her—had departed.

Then, barely had all of their visitors gone, Horace was murmuring that he felt a bit peckish and, since he seemed not to know one end of a bread knife from the other, Taryn was delayed by getting him some supper—and naturally supper for Eva too.

Feeling more ready for her bed than for typing, Taryn eventually had chance to look at the report. There was masses of it! Nor was it an easy report to decipher, she discovered, the fine handwritten scrawl going on for page after endless page.

Feeling more sympathy than her aunt had shown for the typist who had made such a 'dog's breakfast' of it, Taryn finally made it to her bed around three o'clock on Monday morning.

She was up again after a few hours' sleep, and was showered and dressed before she was fully awake. Having promised to deliver the typed report to her aunt's offices on her way to work, Taryn set her car in that direction, feeling like death.

Traffic was heavy, but she got the briefcase to her aunt by eight forty-five, in plenty of time. She was not so fortunate in her timing when she reached her own office.

Kate was not in yet and, Taryn guessed, must be feeling pretty rotten. She was not feeling so chipper herself as she seated herself at her desk. She just did not need to have Jake Nash stroll into her office and look down at her, causing her to have to look up, only to have him grumpily observe, as he noted her pale face and shadowed eyes, 'You look as though you've had a good weekend!'

He was no doubt believing she had spent some extended time with Matt over the weekend. It annoyed her. 'Like you wouldn't believe,' she answered, affecting a pleased smile. Oh, my, that scowl told her that had not gone down well.

'Hmm,' he grunted. 'Didn't take you long to forget Brian Mellor, did it?'

Had she had the energy, Taryn felt she might have stood up and walked out right then. 'Who says I've forgotten him?' she snapped, while at the same time having to concede he was right—it had taken no time at all for her to forget Brian.

'Hmmph!' he snorted, and demanded she find him some paper-work he needed.

Kate came in around ten, looking about as worn out as Taryn felt. Their employer was much more sympathetic to her, however. Taryn felt he was just being deliberately awkward too that, when she did not *want* him looking through from behind his desk straight to hers, he left the door between their offices open.

When for about the fifth time that afternoon she could not hold back a yawn, she was made to weather his sour look. She felt very much like making a face at him when he left his seat and came and closed the door with a very sharp click.

Taryn recovered her equilibrium as the week progressed, and was pleased that her boss seemed to have found his sunnier side. No doubt the fact that Sophie Austin seemed keen on him had something to do with that. She was always phoning him, at any rate, Taryn re-flected, feeling a shade not quite happy about that—though she was sure she didn't give a fig how many Sophies or Louises rang him.

It had been one of the busiest of weeks, and Taryn was not at all sorry when Friday galloped in. No work tomorrow; time to recharge her batteries ready for what would probably be another hectic Monday.

Kate went off shopping when lunch-hour arrived, and Taryn strolled to the canteen. She contemplated having a cooked lunch, but on thinking of her workload settled for a sandwich.

She was on the way back to her desk, however, when she saw Kenton Harris, one of the directors, coming towards her. He was pushing forty and was on his second marriage—rumour being that his second marriage was in trouble. But Taryn believed he was quite harmless.

'How are you getting on?' he enquired, waylaying her.

'I'm enjoying the work very much,' she replied, and would have moved on. She was prevented from doing so when he stretched out a casual arm and rested it on the wall in front of her.

'Good, good!' he commented. She felt it would look quite ridiculous if she did a circuit round him, so stood there calmly waiting for him to move out of her way. 'I've two tickets for the theatre tomorrow,' he said, with his best smile. 'I'd very much like it if you'd come with me? We could—'

Enough was enough. 'Are you married?' she asked, point-blank.

He seemed a little startled, but in his favour answered honestly, 'On the way to getting divorced.'

'Ask me when your divorce is finalised,' she advised him bluntly.

He looked even more startled. 'That's a date!' he declared, and grinned. And for no reason, the whole episode suddenly seeming funny, Taryn found she was smiling back at him.

It was a brief moment of shared humour, but she was more interested in getting back to her desk.

That was when she found that they were not alone in the corridor. Standing there, with Kenton Harris's back towards him, was Jake Nash. A Jake Nash who seemed far from pleased to be observing his temporary PA sharing some joke with one of his directors.

She glanced from him and, silently fuming that the man really did bring out the worst in her sometimes, decided she had no need at all rush back to her desk. Let him think what he would. She was sure she did not care what opinion he had of her.

He had gone the next time she glanced along the corridor. Bubbles to him! She detoured to the cloakroom, and five minutes later felt calmer than she had.

Or so she thought. But no sooner had she made it back to her desk than Jake Nash appeared from nowhere to slam into her. 'You can't resist it, can you?'

She did not care to be spoken to like that, but managed to stay cool, and even say a calm, 'What?'

'Flirting with married men!' he did not hesitate to reply. And, while she stared at him, a trifle stunned, 'Well, let me tell you, Miss Webster,' he rapped, 'I do not pay you to flirt on my time.'

Of all the nerve! All sign of being cool disintegrated. 'It's a moot point if my lunch hour *is* your time!' she flew, before she could hold it back.

Jake Nash's expression hardened. 'You know he's married?' he challenged harshly.

Grief! All she'd done was leave the office for a sandwich! 'I made a point of finding out, naturally,' she tossed back.

'Of course you did!' he snarled. 'What is it with you and married men?' he demanded.

And that made her furious. 'I'd prefer you didn't use what I told you in confidence to have a go at me for no good reason!' she blew indignantly, wishing she had never said a word to him of her love for Brian Mellor.

Jake Nash did not back down on his aggression. 'Tough!' he barked.

Taryn glared at him—and on that happy note Kate, laden with shopping, came in. She looked from one to the other, her atmosphere antennae picking up bad vibes.

'Can I help you with that?' Taryn asked, ignoring Jake and going forward, forcing a smile so Kate might think her antennae were for once faulty.

'I swear I only went out for a couple of things,' she was saying as Jake, obviously wanting no part in this domestic discussion, went to his office and closed the door.

He went off to a meeting at four, but rang through before he went to remind Kate that he would expect her to have left by five.

Kate must have been feeling quite whacked, Taryn realized, when at four forty-five she started clearing her desk. 'Do you need me for anything?' she thought to ask, before gathering up her shopping.

'Everything's fine,' Taryn answered, and, aware how Kate seemed to suffer on her days off, 'Have a better weekend,' she bade her.

Her own weekend promised nothing much to recommend it. She might give Matt a call and see what he was up to, she mused. But, more importantly, she wanted to find some alternative accommodation. More important still, and much more immediate, she wanted to get her own desk cleared, so that she could be out of there before jolly Jake Nash came back from his meeting.

Another minute and she'd have made it too, she fumed when, her desk locked, shoulder bag in hand, the outer door opened and Jake came in. The fact that he had used that particular door told her he wanted a word. It had better be about work. She had not forgiven him for his personal remarks earlier—nor would she in a hurry.

'I was just about to leave,' she stated pointedly, hostilely, setting her bag down on her desk, guessing she was about to switch on her computer again.

To her surprise, though, Jake stood looking at her, serious grey eyes reading the mutiny in warring dark blue eyes. 'I owe you an apology,' he stated.

*Get down on your knees.* She did not feel like making it easy for him. 'Have you realised the error of your ways?' *Beg!*

He shrugged. 'I had a few words with Kenton Harris after the meeting.'

'He obviously told you something of our—flirty—conversation,' she replied acidly, fully expecting him to take exception not only to her words, but to the way she said them.

To surprise her further, he took exception to neither, but revealed, 'Kenton was telling me how glad he would be when his divorce came through—and how you had refused to go out with him. That in effect you had more or less told him to get lost until he was single again.' Jake paused, and then said gently, 'I hurt you, didn't I?'

She did not want his gentle tone, it was weakening. When he was tough she could—outwardly at any rate—be tough back. But showing this unexpected sensitive side was fracturing her.

'You can be very hurtful sometimes,' she told him, the unexpected sting of tears to her eyes giving a hiding to the hard tone she had wanted. She swallowed hard. 'And don't for goodness' sake go all soft on me. You'll have me in tears.'

'Oh, Taryn, I'm sorry,' he apologised, and, just as if he could not help himself, he stretched out a hand to her cheek. And as if he had spotted the shine of tears in her eyes, 'don't cry!' he said urgently. 'Please don't cry.'

And at his tone, the genuine regret, the fear that he was the cause of her tears, the touch of his fingers gentle on her cheek, all Taryn's determination to not yield an inch evaporated.

'I wouldn't dream of crying on you,' she answered, a smile appearing for the first time.

Then all at once, as she stared up at him, something in his expression changed and, as though he could not stop himself, Jake Nash bent down and gently, tenderly, placed his lips over hers.

Stunned, she stood stock still. But abruptly, as if only then alive to what he was doing—and appalled by his own actions—Jake pulled rapidly back. 'I shouldn't have done that!' he exclaimed, his voice shocked, as though he himself barely knew what had come over him. 'Oh, hell…'

But even while something pretty momentous was happening in Taryn—to be perfectly honest she had not minded his kiss one bit, and in point of fact would quite welcome another—she knew what he was saying. He was her boss, and in his view he had just breached the very first rule of the employer-employee relationship. You just did not go around kissing your staff.

'I'll forgive you. Thousands wouldn't,' she offered brightly. And just had to jibe, when he still looked as if he was having trouble believing what, probably for the first time in his professional life he had done, 'See where a guilty conscience will get you?'

He smiled then. 'You'd better go home, Taryn,' he suggested gruffly. 'There's something about you…' He left it there, and with barely a goodnight Taryn picked up her bag and got out of there.

His kiss had been electrifying. His kiss, that had barely been a

kiss at all, had set all kinds of mind-blowing sensations and imaginings off into orbit within her.

Her last office employer had kissed her and she, believing she
loved him, had bolted out of there from fear that she might respond.
Jake—Jake had kissed her just now. A kiss that was not a lover's
kiss, or even a would-be lover's kiss. And yet somehow she was
finding the experience far more earth-shattering!

# CHAPTER FOUR

IT TOOK Taryn most of the weekend to get herself back together from the unexpectedness of Jake's kiss. Not that it could properly be called a kiss—though she did not know what else to call it. She supposed it had been more a meeting of lips, his and hers, but, oh, the feelings it had set off inside her!

She had driven home in a daze. How on earth—when she had believed she loved Brian Mellor, and the jury was still out on whether or not she liked Jake Nash—had Jake's kiss somehow seemed far more devastating than Brian's?

She had still been inwardly shaking when she'd reached her home. Like him, not like him, and once feeling so angry with him that she could have hit him, Taryn had been glad to have the kitchen to herself as she tried to analyse the weird effect her present boss had on her.

He—disturbed her. Yes, that was it. He disturbed her. With Brian, her office relationship with him—until that very last day— had gone along plain sailing, with never a ripple in their working relationship. With Jake, ripples could be gigantic emotional waves on an instant.

And yet when she had been so out of sorts with him that she had barely wanted to say a word to him, Jake had revealed that wonderful, well-hidden, sensitive side. And she had come over all weepy because of it. And he—he had kissed her. And, to be quite honest, she did not know where the Dickens she was.

But she knew she should not read anything into any of it. Kate had told her quite plainly that day she had taken her around to meet some of her co-workers that Jake had no room for 'that sort of entanglement' in his business life.

By Monday Taryn had got herself into one piece. And by Monday, too, she knew—if she hadn't already—what Jake's 'Oh, hell' had been all about. It had sprung from the fact that he had just crossed the bounds of what was acceptable in a working relationship.

He was pleasant that Monday, but cool. Communicative, but detached. And that was fine by her. All too obviously he regretted having kissed her. In all honesty, Taryn could not say the same. She was glad she had seen that more sensitive side of him—albeit that he was keeping it very well hidden now.

But all too evidently he wanted everything back on a business footing. And she would not have it any other way. 'I'll leave these for your signature,' she told him efficiently, courteously, and with a smile that did not reach her eyes.

'Book a table for two for Saturday,' he instructed.

So who's the lucky girl? A dart of what could not possibly be jealousy momentarily wiped the smile from her face. 'The Almora?' Taryn queried, and immediately pinned another smile on her mouth, to convey that he could dine with both Louise, Sophie and their mothers too, for that matter, for all she cared.

She hoped the Almora, one of his favourite watering holes of the moment, was full, with no chance of a table, and was half minded when she phoned not to say who the table was required for. Mention of Jake Nash's name got him a table straight away of course.

Taryn felt then that she wouldn't mind if he took himself off to some meeting or other. She felt fidgety, somehow, to know that he was in the next-door office.

Yet when on Tuesday he announced he would be out of the

office from tomorrow until the following Monday, that he had several days' business overseas, that did not suit Taryn either.

He had only been gone a few hours, yet by eleven on Wednesday she—unbelievably—realised that she was missing him. Somehow life without him around had lost its edge.

Kate started to go down with a cold that day too. 'Why don't you go home?' Taryn urged.

'I wouldn't mind,' Kate replied, but got hung up on something and was still there at five.

She struggled into the office on Thursday, but looked so poorly Taryn could not bear it. 'Oh, please go home,' she pressed. 'There's nothing here you need to worry about.'

Kate hesitated. Devoted to her job though she was, her greater concern was for her baby—and bed had much more appeal than the office just then. 'You're sure you can cope?'

'Yes, of course,' Taryn answered confidently. Only she would know the reservations she had about that.

'You'll ring me if you have any problems?'

'There won't be any, I promise,' Taryn replied. And from the moment Kate went home, she did not have a minute to breathe. How on earth Kate had coped on her own, when she was the only PA in the office, Taryn did not know. She supposed that when Kate had been fit and well, prior to conceiving her much longed for child, she had been one of those genius kind of women who took everything in their stride and simply ate work.

Hoping to prove at the end of her year there that she might have grown into a PA somewhere approaching Kate's standard, Taryn worked through her lunch hour. She knew she would be working late that night too.

It was around four-thirty, however, when the phone rang. 'Mr Nash's office?' she responded.

'Busy?' asked a voice that for some unknown reason made her feel all fluttery inside.

With Jake's cool tone of Monday and Tuesday gone, Taryn knew that she liked him. 'Managing to earn my corn,' she answered, a smile there in her voice.

'You more than do that, Miss Webster,' he replied, his tone friendly.

'Thank you, Mr Nash,' she returned, and waited in the pause that followed for him to say why he was ringing.

'Put Kate on, will you?' he requested after a moment.

'Er—Kate's not around just now,' Taryn replied. Time enough for him to know on Monday that Kate had gone off sick. No point in having him thinking that the office had collapsed with its two main functionaries absent.

'Where is she?' he asked. And, not waiting for an answer, 'Is she unwell?'

'She—um—has a cold,' Taryn replied, as in all honesty, since he was the big chief, she saw she had to.

If she had seen that, though, she was starting to think that he saw much, much more. Because, either picking up on her small hesitation or too shrewd by half, 'Kate's not in, is she?' he demanded to know.

'She came in, but she looked so washed out, and obviously felt it, that I urged her to go home.'

His pleasant tone was back when, 'Good for you,' he approved. Taryn felt warm all over. 'Any problems?'

'Not one,' she assured him.

'You're sure you can manage on your own?'

'Absolutely,' she responded cheerfully.

'Then I'll see you Monday,' he said, and was gone.

Taryn spent a few minutes of precious work time wondering when he would be coming home. He was dining at the Almora on Saturday—she didn't care to know with whom—so would probably be flying in some time on Saturday morning.

As she had anticipated, Taryn worked late that night. She was happy to do so. She loved the work she did. She had wanted a job, a career she could get stuck into. This was it. She only hoped that when Kate returned from maternity leave, and she had to move on, she would find something she loved equally.

Taryn had barely arrived home that night before her cousin Matt came round to see her. 'I need a favour,' he said straight off.

'Name it,' she offered without hesitation.

'I've been getting a few "poor guy—he's been dumped" kind of looks from one or two in the office. I want a pretty girl on my arm for the firm's dinner-dance.'

'I'm elected?' she asked, her heart aching for him. He was good-looking, and a lovely person, and she was sure there must be half a dozen women who would love to go out with him. But he considered himself still married and, wanting Alison back, either thought it unfair on anyone to date them, or plain just had no interest in dating.

'Will you?' he asked.

'Of course I will. I'd love to. When is it?'

'Tomorrow.'

*'Matthew Kiteley!'* she scolded.

'I know, I know—short notice. But I was going to go on my own—and then I spotted the "poor bloke" looks—and, well...'

'What time?'

'Seven.'

Oh, crumbs. Jake would be in the office before her on Monday. There would be no time to catch up on anything she had left undone before he arrived. And after her 'Absolutely' answer to him when he had asked if she was sure she could manage, it was a matter of pride that she cleared her desk before she left the office tomorrow evening.

'You can't come?' Matt asked, seeing from her expression that something was bothering her. 'You've got something else on tomorrow?'

'It isn't that,' she answered quickly, and explained, 'I know this will sound silly, but I'm in the office on my own tomorrow, and Fridays are always busy.' The way Kate had been looking, there was no way she would be fit to come to work tomorrow. 'It's a sort of honour thing that I clear my work before I leave.'

Matt knew her well enough to not think it silly at all. He was, after all, of the same highly principled clan. 'You think you'll be working late?' he documented.

There was no 'think' about it, and normally she would not have cared how late she stayed at her desk. 'I could probably be through around half past six,' she calculated.

'You won't have time to drive home, change your clothes and be ready for me to pick you up,' he said, but as ever, after a few moments' thought, found the solution. 'How about I pick you up from your office? You can take your clobber with you in the morning and change there.' He had a better idea. 'And to save you taking your car I could call here for you in the morning,' he continued, working it out as he went along. 'We'll probably have to leave here a bit earlier to get both you and me to work on time. What do you think?'

Poor Matt. She just could not bear the thought of his work colleagues pitying him at the dinner-dance because he did not have a partner. 'A majestic plan,' she said with a grin. 'Though I can't say that I'll be ready at exactly six-thirty.'

'That's all right. I expect—except for security staff—most of your people will be gone by then. I'll park on your forecourt and wait. We needn't bother with the pre-dinner chit-chat. As long as we're there to sit down at seven-thirty it won't matter.'

Taryn spent time before going to bed in looking out what she would wear tomorrow night. For Matt's sake she wanted to look her best.

As agreed, he called for her early the following morning, and hung her dress carrier in his car. 'I'll be here at a quarter to seven,' he said as they parted, adding, 'You know you're a pearl among women!'

'Yeah, yeah,' she laughed, and hurried into the building.

Since Jake wasn't in, and she did not want her dress on display for all who wandered in, she took it, and the bag with her shoes, fresh underwear and toiletries, through to his cloakroom and left her dress hanging in there.

As she had anticipated, Kate did not come in to work. She rang though, her voice so thick with cold as she asked if everything was okay that Taryn knew she was feeling worse rather than better.

'Don't worry about a thing except getting well,' she answered. 'I'm on top of everything, I promise.'

She managed to get to the staff canteen to purchase a sandwich at lunchtime, and then put her head down and worked solidly through. With luck she would have chance to catch her breath on the drive from her office to the dinner-dance venue.

At six twenty-five, with quite a glow of satisfaction, Taryn surveyed her cleared desk and, not wanting to keep her cousin waiting, hurried to retrieve her dress and belongings.

It had been her intention to go along to the staff cloakroom to spruce up a little and change, but, feeling hot from the urgency of her labours, and a little grubby, her eyes lit on Jake's shower.

*No,* said that part of her that knew right from wrong. Why not? said that part of her that had worked hard, fast and furiously for him that day. She knew he had a meeting planned for nine-thirty on Monday. She could take the towel she used home, give it a wash, and bring it back Monday, pop it back in while he was at his meeting. He would never know.

Before she could argue further, Taryn, her blonde hair piled on top of her head, was in the shower. It was bliss, reviving, and she knew she would feel more like partying afterwards.

But she knew she should not stay showering for long. Even now, Matt was probably pulling up outside to wait for her. Feeling very much refreshed, she stepped from the shower and—having not heard anyone come in—very nearly went into heart failure!

With her only covering an instant searing and hot blush, Taryn stood stunned. 'You... You shouldn't...' she gasped, feeling scarlet from head to toe, too shaken rigid to move, too stunned to even find sufficient wit to consider what Jake Nash was doing there when he should be thousands of miles away.

He seemed equally shaken. But, for all his grey eyes swept appreciatively over her naked figure, he was the first to recover. 'I should get some clothes on if I were you,' he suggested smoothly. 'You'll catch your death, trotting around like that.'

Never had she ever felt so boilingly hot. But even before she could move a half-step Jake was calmly reaching for the towel and handing it to her. Without another word he strolled out and left her to dry herself—and get some clothes on!

Regardless of the time going on, of Matt waiting for her, Taryn had to take a few minutes to just stand there and try to gather some sense of normality. It was an impossible task.

How in the world was she going to face Jake Nash again? Was he in his office waiting for her to come out? Oh, Lord! The fact that she had made use of his private bathroom was not then the issue. What bothered her was that he, Jake, had come in and found his temporary assistant stark naked, stitchless, the only thing covering her—her blushes!

Taryn dried herself and started to dress, applied the small amount of make-up she wore, and let down her hair, hoping, with all she had, that Jake had made a tactful retreat.

While there was obviously no reason why he should do anything of the sort—he had clearly returned to the office on a point of business—she felt, if luck was with her, that the best thing that could happen would be if he had left the building. That way she would not have to see him until Monday. That was should she have found the nerve by then to actually *come* back.

With a sudden urgent awareness of Matt waiting outside, and an awareness that it was important to him that they were sitting down to dinner at seven-thirty, she left the bathroom.

With the suit she had worn that day on a hanger in one hand, the carrier of shoes and other belongings in the other, she went into Jake's office—and knew her luck had run out!

Jake was sitting at his desk. He was not working—but waiting. She went crimson again as his glance, taking in her high colour, went over her strapless red dress, close-fitting at the bust, with a full skirt that ended just below her knees.

He got to his feet. She was wearing higher heels than she normally wore—she still had to look up to him. 'I—don't know what to say,' she said, in a voice all husky and full of nerves.

'You're obviously out on the tiles tonight,' he observed.

'I didn't have time to go home and change.'

'I managed to work that out for myself,' Jake answered dryly.

Taryn felt a spurt of annoyance with him. 'I'd better go. Matt's waiting for me outside.'

Jake looked a shade disgruntled. 'I suppose I must be thankful you didn't invite him up to scrub your back,' he replied curtly.

Again Taryn felt an urge to hit him. What *was* it about this man? 'I'd better go,' she repeated coolly, and went to the door.

To her surprise, Jake walked with her. Not only that, but as they waited for the lift he took the suit hanger from her. She was, she conceded, rather burdened, but could have managed.

They stepped into the lift when it came, and she realised that he must have completed whatever task he had come in for. The lift was on its way down when, having decided not to speak to him again unless she had to, she suddenly realised something. 'I forgot the towel!' she exclaimed.

'I'm not with you?'

'The towel I used. I was going to take it home and launder it, and bring it back Monday.'

'And I would never have known?' he mocked. *Oh, one of these days!* 'I shouldn't worry about it,' he advised. 'Housekeeping will see to it.'

The lift arrived at the ground floor and the doors opened. 'Goodnight,' she bade him, turning to take the hanger from him. He did not answer. Nor did he hand over the hanger.

Taryn found he was crossing the foyer with her. Now, by the look of it, she was going to have to introduce her cousin to him.

One of the security men stepped forward and opened the doors for them. It was a lovely evening, and still daylight. Taryn saw Matt straight away. He saw them too, and at once stepped out from his car.

'I'm sorry to have kept you waiting,' she apologised.

'You're well worth waiting for,' he answered gallantly, and kissed her cheek.

'This is my boss, Jake Nash.' She had no option but to perform the introduction. 'Matthew Kiteley,' she completed. She had been going to add *my cousin,* but as the two men shook hands and Matt relieved Jake of the hanger it suddenly became unthinkable that Jake Nash should know that, come Friday evening in swinging London, she should be going out with her cousin—as if she couldn't get a date with any other male.

Which was, she fully accepted as she and Matt drove along, totally absurd. He—Jake—knew of at least two other men who had wanted to date her.

The evening was a huge success. Matt introduced her round, but did not mention that they were cousins. And when afterwards he drove her home it was to comment, 'Thanks, Taryn. With your magnificent help I think I've seen the last of those looks of commiseration.'

Taryn had a feeling he was over-sensitive. As far as she could tell everyone she had met seemed to hold Matt in very high regard. 'Any time, love,' she said, as they kissed cheeks and he watched her indoors.

Any time, she mused as she went upstairs to bed. Although, no matter how short of time she was, she would never be using that particular shower again.

She set about seriously trying to find somewhere else to live on

Saturday. But owned she was not truly in a mood for flat hunting. Time and again flashes of Jake Nash walking in on her as she made full use of his facilities would come back to haunt her.

That she was unsuccessful in her accommodation hunt was not as upsetting as it might otherwise have been. More importantly was the worry—did she owe Jake an apology? Had she in fact already apologised? She could not remember. That did not surprise her. What was uppermost in her memory was the way he had casually ambled in and she, like a rabbit caught in the headlights, had just stood there while he had looked his fill as she stood there naked to the world! She blushed now just to think of it.

Taryn still did not know what to do about an apology when she went into the office on Monday. She was thankful to see that Kate was in—not because of the workload, but because it limited the one-to-one time she would have to spend with Jake.

Kate, though still looking peaky, was much improved. But, perhaps because their employer was striving not to overburden her that day, it was Taryn he called in when he had some dictation to give.

She decided against the apology. Decided that the moment had passed when she should bring the subject up. But no sooner was she seated, pen and pad at the ready and looking for him to start, than she realised that *he* was not ready yet.

He returned her glance—she felt a tide of hot colour rise to her face. Her high colour seemed to hold his attention for a moment, and then he was commenting, 'I take it you enjoyed your evening on Friday?'

Oh, grief! 'I'm s-sorry—about that.' She found she was stammering before she could stop herself. 'Your shower, I mean.'

'It was—hmm—quite a—revelation,' he murmured lightly. And she coloured again, because she knew from the sudden wicked gleam in his eyes that he was referring to the way she had revealed herself in all her nakedness.

'It won't happen again,' she stated primly.

And he smiled as he replied, 'Now, how did I already know that?'

She refused to answer, and gave him a cold look to convey that as far as she was concerned this conversation was over, and that if he had any dictation to give then it was about time he started.

Pointedly, she looked down to her pad, pen poised. Then discovered that he was the one in charge, not she. He was the one who would decide when he started, and he was not the smallest bit impressed by her cold look. 'So, what's with you and Matthew Kiteley?' he questioned coolly.

Her head shot up. There was no sign of a smile about him now. 'What do you mean?' She had no idea where there were at now.

'I had an impression married men were wasting their time with you until their divorce came through,' he enlightened her, adding, 'Kiteley is still wearing his wedding ring.'

Trust him to spot that. 'He wouldn't want to run the risk of forgetting to put it back on before he went back home,' she replied, by then ready to let Nash the Terrible think what the devil he liked.

'To Martin and Black...' he rapped, before she was ready, and shot off page after page of such rapid dictation that her pen fairly flew over the paper.

Ooh, that man, she fumed, as she typed back what she had taken down. She would be glad when he went abroad again!

Or so she'd thought. She had to rethink that idea when on Wednesday—having once again got her to book him a table for two for Saturday, at the Raven this time—he told her he had meetings in Italy on Thursday and Friday. Good! Even though she had to own that there was a part of her that felt a bit out of sorts at the idea of him not being there. *Good!*

'Would you like me to make your hotel reservation?' she enquired.

'If you would,' he agreed. 'Kate knows where I like to stay,' he informed her. And, straight away causing Taryn's spirits to take the most peculiar nosedive, 'You'd better reserve two rooms,' he added.

'Two?' she questioned, before she could stop herself, the most awful sensation of sickness invading her—though she was sure she did not give a button which Louise or Sophie, Mary or Matilda he took with him. More surprising, though, was that he would bother with the extra room!

'Two,' he confirmed. And, to absolutely floor her, 'I'd prefer you to have your own room, if you don't mind.'

Taryn wasn't sure which bit to take exception to first. 'You should be so lucky!' she flew, before, 'I'm coming with you—*to Italy?*' she exclaimed.

'Kate isn't up to it,' he responded shortly, and Taryn knew then that not only would he prefer she had a room of her own, but that he would by far prefer to have Kate with him on this trip.

Kate had mentioned at her interview that she occasionally flew abroad with Jake on business. But Taryn hadn't given thought to the fact that *she* might be called upon to go in her stead. She took a deep breath, put her best PA hat on, and decided to show him that she was not going to make a fuss and was entirely unfazed that he had dropped this on her at such short notice. 'We'll be back by Friday evening?' she enquired.

'Why—have you some other married man champing at the bit?' Jake asked nastily.

And there had she been, thinking him sensitive! 'I'm saving him for Saturday,' she replied sweetly. 'Is there anything else?'

'Kate will fill you in,' he grated, and Taryn went back to her desk wondering—did she really, really want this job?

Her head was swimming by the time she left her office that night. Kate had seen to the hotel reservations and—since this was a working trip—had suggested she take the office laptop with her. She had also arranged for her to have anything else she might need installed in her room. 'Jake sometimes likes to read through anything you have ready on the return flight,' she had enlightened her. 'So anything you manage to type back would be useful.'

'You'll be all right on your own?' Taryn had asked.

'Bless you.' Kate had smiled. 'Jake has said if I feel at all below par to get Dianne Farmer in here to do the donkey work.' By then Taryn was aware that Dianne Farmer was not the most favourite apple in Kate's particular barrel, and guessed that Kate would have to be very much below par—on her knees, in fact—before she would call Dianne in.

But by the time she reached her home that night Taryn knew that she really, really *did* want this job. She loved the buzz, the work, and, yes, when he wasn't acting like a bear with a boil in his ear, she most often liked Jake. Besides which, apart from the loyalty she owed to Kate, Taryn wanted that career. And nowhere would she get more fully rounded career experience than working in the office she was in.

She made a meal for her father and stepmother, then went up to pack an overnight bag. When she drove to the airport the next morning she was wearing a suit of deep blue that seemed to bring a more violet shade of colour to her eyes.

'Taryn,' Jake greeted her affably when he saw his, his glance flicking over her. 'Feeling sharp?'

She didn't know about that. What she did know was that *he* was looking sharp—not to mention handsome, worldly, sophisticated. And, with her heart suddenly going nineteen to the dozen, she was beginning to feel a little out of her depth.

They went straight to their hotel once their plane had landed, but stayed only long enough to drop off their overnight cases—where Taryn discovered she had a very large and light room. From there they were chauffeured to the Bergoni company, and from then on it was work, work and more work. There was a break for lunch, where Jake sat still talking business with the head of the company, and she sat a few places down on the opposite side, next to Signor Bergoni's PA—a male in his late twenties who was introduced to her as Franco Causio and who, while keeping a keen eye on business, managed to find space to ask her out that evening.

'I'm afraid I'll be busy,' she replied, and caught the brief but definitely displeased glint in Jake's eyes as he chose that moment to look her way. Grief, the man missed *nothing!*

As was proved on the journey back to their hotel later that afternoon. 'Were you making arrangement to see Causio?' he asked straight out, not sounding too thrilled.

Would I dare? 'I hope you don't mind—I turned him down,' she said nicely. 'I wasn't sure it would be appropriate.'

'Because we've been talking contracts?'

'I told him I'd be busy.'

'If I'm not mistaken, he suggested you could join him afterwards—perhaps take a later dinner?'

His tone had mellowed. She smiled at him. 'Not much gets by you does it?' she answered lightly. And felt good inside suddenly.

They parted at the hotel—he to go to his room, she to go to hers. She guessed he would be using his room as an office and would already have his briefcase opened. She supposed she should make a start on typing back the scads of notes she had taken too, but... Her bed looked tempting. She had worked hard too that day.

Taryn slipped out of her suit and donned a wrap—and could not ignore the invitation to put her feet up. Just five minutes, then she would switch the computer on and get busy.

She lay on top of her bed, considering that, all in all, she was rather pleased with her first 'foreign assignment'. She admitted a warm glow of pride as she recalled how, when Signor Bergoni had asked after Signora Lambert's wellbeing, Jake had explained that Kate was indisposed and had introduced her as, 'Signorina Webster, a senior PA and Signora Lambert's most efficient deputy.'

Taryn found she was inwardly smiling when she thought of Jake. Apart from that small hiccup when he had not liked the idea that Franco Causio was asking her out—and that had been purely because Jake was guarding his business—they had got on well. She hoped he wasn't still wishing it was Kate he had with him and not her. She closed her eyes. He…

Taryn woke up an hour later and just could not believe that not only had she fallen asleep, but she had slept for *a whole hour!*

However, no need to panic. She had a lot of work to type back, true. But she had the rest of the evening to complete it. She went and had a leisurely shower, washing her hair while she was about it. Then, seeing no point in getting dressed again, she put on some underwear and once more donned her wrap. She dried her hair and was then ready to start work again.

An hour later she was making inroads into her typing when the sound of someone at her door buzzer make her jump.

Leaving what she was doing, she went to answer it. Jake stood there—and all of a sudden she felt shy! It was because of what she was wearing, she told herself, because of the informality of her attire. But he had seen her in less.

'Hello,' she said, her voice wretchedly husky.

'Taryn.' Just her name—his way of saying hello as his eyes raked over her. And unexpectedly, almost as if the moment had caught him off-guard too, 'You're so beautiful,' he said softly. And her heart kicked off a riot.

But she knew at once that he was already regretting what he would consider a most unprofessional remark—it was there in the way he pulled back from the door. There in the sudden stiff look of him.

She searched for some light remark, so he would know she had not taken him seriously. 'I'll arrange your eye-test when we get back, shall I?'

The stiffness went from him. He relaxed, even laughed. 'I'm ready for dinner. How long will it take you?' he asked.

Taryn stared at him. After the monster lunch she had eaten, she had not given dinner a thought. But by the look of it Jake was expecting her to join him for dinner.

'I'm not hungry,' she answered, her heartbeats acting up again. Suddenly she would like nothing better than to have dinner with him.

'You must eat,' Jake told her.

Oh, how she wished she had not said she was not hungry! 'No, really,' she felt forced to continue. 'If I feel hungry later I'll have Room Service send something up. In any case, I've some work to complete, and I'd much sooner get on with that.'

He looked a touch taken aback by that. She guessed that it wasn't every day that one of his dinner invitations got turned down, albeit in favour of doing his work. 'As you please,' he answered, and left her to it.

It was an age, though, before she felt in the mood to start typing again. Jake thought her beautiful, she mused dreamily. Standing there, with not a scrap of make-up on, her hair all any-old-how, he'd thought her beautiful. And she had refused to have dinner with him! Too late now.

Taryn owned she was experiencing some very peculiar sensations when she was near him. She had just got herself back together again when her phone rang. It was Room Service.

'Signor Nash has said you wish to order?' enquired a charming voice—and she went all soft inside again. Even though that more logical part of her said that Jake must be thinking she would be useless to him as a personal assistant if she fainted away from lack of nourishment, she could not help but think how dear of him it was to think of her.

Dear! Oh, for goodness' sake! Buck your ideas up, she scolded. 'Um—a cheese sandwich and some coffee would be good,' she answered, suddenly realising that the poor man was waiting for her order.

Jake, the 'dear' man of the previous evening, seemed at pains to show her the next morning that there had been nothing remotely personal in either his 'beautiful' remark or in his action in making sure she was fed. While she could not fault his manners when anyone else was around, he could not have been colder to her had he tried.

And that suited her fine. Dear! She must have been off her head! It must have been the charm of Italy getting to her. Not that she had seen much of it. Airport, the flash of streets as they raced by, the Bergoni headquarters and the hotel just about summed up the trip.

Nor had she seen anything more than that of Italy when, around four that afternoon, they made their way to the airport again. She had already handed over the wedge of papers she had typed the evening before, and had a pad full of matter to be typed back as soon as she reached her desk on Monday. But, so much for her typing efforts, Jake preferred to spend the flight writing up notes of his own. Since he had not thawed out at all, she was glad that she had the next two days off, and would not have to have anything more to do with him until Monday.

'You have transport home?' he unbent sufficiently to enquire when they landed.

She would have said yes even if it had meant she'd have to walk it. 'Yes, thank you,' she replied primly, and knew that his eyes were on her. But she had something better to do than look at him.

'Thank you for your help this last couple of days.' He unbent a little further.

She could feel herself weakening, and did not want to. 'It's what I'm paid for,' she replied civilly. If he wanted a smile to go with that—tough. She left him with a stiff goodbye.

On her drive home she acknowledged that she felt well and truly not her normal self—and it did not take much analysing. It was *him*, of course. Though why he should have the power he did over her emotions was something of a mystery. Other than it was only natural, surely, that she would prefer to work in perfect harmony.

By good fortune, when there had been no word of it yesterday, her stepmother had engaged a new housekeeper. Mrs Ferris, a fierce-looking woman, who looked as if she would not take any prisoners, was already established in the household when Taryn got in. Taryn could see many a battle ahead between the two; Mrs Ferris did not seem as if she would put up with any nonsense from the lady of the house!

The new housekeeper's existence, however, made Taryn's life easier. She had time on Saturday morning to check over the notes she had taken down yesterday. And was in actual fact still studying them when her aunt Hilary rang.

'Doing anything special tonight?' Hilary Kiteley asked, after they had exchanged warm greetings. 'I know you're off the hook housekeeping-wise.'

'You've heard about Mrs Ferris?'

'I found her for you. A formidable lady. Too good to waste on anyone other than Eva.'

'You're incorrigible!' Taryn laughed.

'I'm in trouble.'

'What? Can I help?'

'You can. It's a bit of a cheek but… Well, I need a hotel receptionist for a few hours tonight. It's only for a few hours,' she repeated. 'Only, well, it doesn't seem to be worth anyone's effort to turn out for just a few hours. And I kind of promised—' She broke off—and just waited.

Oh, Auntie! Taryn knew that she did not want the job either. She had her career. She didn't want to do anything else. And certainly not temp work as well as a full-time and exacting job.

But that was when, even while knowing all of that, family loyalty kicked in. Add to that that she loved her aunt—plus the fact that when her mother had left her aunt had always been there for her. And with her aunt giving her no pressure, the only pressure coming from within herself, Taryn accepted that she did not have a choice.

'You know that I haven't the first idea of what a hotel receptionist does?'

'It won't be a problem,' Hilary answered. And, relief evident in her voice, she went on to explain how the Irwin Hotel had a huge function booked for that evening but had been badly affected by a flu outbreak. Staff had been phoning in sick all week, and while she had been able to help them out with waitresses and kitchen assistants, Mr Buckley, the manager, needed someone presentable and with a good manner to stand in at reception.

'That's all I've got to do for a few hours?' Taryn queried.

'All—I promise. Probably hand out keys and book people in. Though at that time of night they're not expecting hordes of new arrivals—well, apart from the people attending this function. It's a big dinner thing, apparently, so you may have to point guests in the direction of that room too—though it's bound to be signposted.'

Taryn couldn't see it being that simple. 'Will I have someone with me?'

'There's a junior who hasn't gone down with flu. She'll be able to show you the ropes. But you shouldn't have to do very much at all. I wouldn't ask you, but, having found them a load of other staff, the receptionist stumped me.'

Taryn said goodbye to her aunt, having received details of the address, but she could not say she was looking forward to the evening. Then she felt exceedingly mean. After the way her aunt had always looked out for her. She had been the one, too, who had found her that job with dear Osgood Compton. If Aunt Hilary had not done that, Taryn reasoned, she would never have met Jake Nash and…Jake was in her head. He seemed to be pretty much a fixture there just lately, she reflected.

The phone rang again during the afternoon. Anticipating it might be her aunt with more instructions, Taryn picked it up and said, 'Hello,' and got the shock of her life. It was Jake Nash!

'I need you over here,' he said without preamble.

Pardon? 'At the office?' she asked, with no intention whatsoever of going.

'My home,' he answered briefly. 'There's something not right with that typing you did—it's not scanning right. I want to go over it with you.'

Honestly! Though—he worked hard all week too—and was still working now! Did he never stop? Well, she knew he did; he was having dinner at the Raven that evening to her certain knowledge.

'I double checked it!' she protested, not wanting to go. Yet at the same time a weird kind of compulsion to drop whatever she was doing—which wasn't a lot—and go and see him came over her.

'Well, you must have missed something.'

Taryn felt sure she had missed nothing—but had to admit that after an action-packed day she had been pretty exhausted by the time she had finished working on Thursday night.

'I'll try and get to you,' she responded. She knew, with the whopping salary he paid her, that she was obliged to—leave alone that being at his beck and call was all part and parcel of a senior PA's lot.

'You'll *try?*'

He was sounding tough, and she hated him. But she wasn't in any hurry to give in easily. 'How long do you think it will take?' she asked, a touch belligerently it had to be said—there was yards of typing to check through!

'As long as it takes.' he retorted crisply. And, mockery there, 'But no need to bring your toothbrush.'

He could go whistle! She had to be at the Irwin Hotel by seven. She knew his address without having to ask. She put down the phone—then picked it up again.

As a precaution, she rang her aunt. 'Something's come up,' she began, and went on to state, 'There shouldn't be a problem.' His table at The Raven was booked for eight, so they'd have finished long before then, 'But there's a very remote possibility I might be a little late getting to the Irwin Hotel. I'll definitely be there, but just in case…'

'I'll ring Mr Buckley and let him know,' her aunt said. 'I'd like him to know that Just Temps is a very reliable agency.'

Taryn, her briefcase and the office laptop on the seat beside her, a black calf-length straight skirt reposing on the back seat of her car, a crisp white shirt hanging up, was feeling a veritable conglomeration of mixed emotions as she drove to Jake's home. She didn't want to go and see him—yet knew that for a lie. Somehow she felt drawn to him—even if at the present time she hated him!

His house was in a smart part of London. Elegant and charming. It took her twenty minutes to find somewhere to park. He answered the door and invited, 'Come in.' And, as they went along the hall, 'Can I get you something to drink?' he thought to enquire.

It was getting on for five by then. She wanted, needed, to be in and out. 'No, thanks,' she refused. 'I'd rather get on.'

'Didn't you advise your date that you'd be late?' Jake asked, in her opinion none too pleasantly.

'He'll wait,' she said sweetly.

His reply was some sort of a grunt as he took her to his study. And from then on it was heads down, she reading back her shorthand while he checked what she had typed.

They were coming to the end when, 'Ah!' he murmured, and showed her where the wording, if altered slightly, made a world of difference to the meaning—although it was her view that their lawyers would have picked that up without their efforts. But who was she to complain?

After instructing her to retype it, Jake stood up and, checking his watch, 'I have to shower and change. If you'd like to make yourself a sandwich…' he began.

'That would put me off my dinner,' she interrupted him pleasantly, inwardly fuming. He knew what he could do with his sandwich! She checked her own watch. How had it got to be six-thirty? Grief, she'd have to get her skates on.

'If you're sure,' he murmured, and strolled out.

Retype it, the *whole* of it! Did she have news for him! She reached for the office laptop, got busy with plugs, and inside another twenty minutes she had the last seven pages amended and reprinted, and the whole document put back together again—and had no time to hang about.

Leaving the document where he could not fail to see it, she replaced her notes inside her briefcase and snapped it shut. She left without stopping to say goodbye, but with all speed just got out of there.

Taryn arrived at the Irwin Hotel at twenty past seven. Skirt and shirt in hand, she hurried in, only to find there were already two people on the reception desk. A senior person, who turned out to be Mrs Buckley, the manager's wife, and the junior her aunt had spoken of.

'I'm so sorry I'm late,' Taryn apologised, thinking it more busi-nesslike not to mention she was related to the head of Just Temps, but explaining she was there to relieve at Reception. 'But you look as though you've got Reception covered and won't need me.'

'We didn't think you were coming—but we need all the help we can get,' Mrs Buckley replied. 'One of Mrs Kiteley's waitresses has let us down.' And, quite out of the blue, 'Ever done any wait-ressing?'

Oh, Auntie, the things I do for you! Before she knew it, Taryn had been taken into the back office, was black-skirted and white-shirted, supplied with a long crisp white apron, had been inspected and passed muster, and had been assigned to a station in the ban-queting room.

She was rusty, but the ins and outs of waitressing soon came back to her. The room was crowded. Mainly business people, she thought, but did not have time to look around.

That was, she did not have time to look around until after the first course had been served and she and her fellow waiters and waitresses went to stand at their various positions in the vast room, ready to be on hand should any of the diners require anything.

Otherwise they were to wait to be signalled to clear away and deliver the next course.

And that was when, having checked that her own diners required nothing, Taryn let her eyes wander around the room. And that was when shock, like a lightning bolt, slammed into her. Her eyes widened, stayed wide and horror-struck, and seemed incapable of moving on. Transfixed, she stared at one of the diners in particular—a diner who was paying not the smallest attention whatsoever to his meal, but who was staring totally thunderstruck straight back at her!

He was, her stunned brain was telling her, the same man with whom she had shared a study not two hours ago! It was—Jake Nash! And he was looking as if he could not believe what his eyes were telling him either.

Wrenching her gaze from him, it crossed Taryn's mind that this would be a good time to faint. Only that would have drawn more attention to her. What was he doing *here?* He should be at the Raven!

Wanting to run, Taryn knew that she could not. There was her aunt's business reputation to consider. Besides which, the people she was working with were a nice bunch and should she make a bolt for it—as every instinct compelled—the extra work, when they were already stretched, would fall on them.

She could only be grateful that she had not been allocated to wait at his table, but still reeling in shock, and knowing that there were going to be repercussions for her from tonight's work, she steeled herself to stay put.

Still mentally staggering, she helped serve the remainder of the dinner. It was when coffee was being served and the dinner guests started milling around that Taryn felt a more urgent need to go and hide. Everything in her urged her to make a break for it then, but it would still fall on the rest of her temporary colleagues to do the clearing up afterwards.

She had just finished the last of her coffee round, and was

about to go to the kitchens when a voice she knew so well said quietly in her ear, 'So now I know the sort of thing you get up to at the weekends!'

Taryn, her insides churning, braved a glance up. Jake Nash was surveying her evenly, but those steady grey eyes were telling her nothing.

Without a word she walked away from him, heading for the kitchens. He did not follow her. She had known that he wouldn't. Just as she also knew that that was not the end of the matter.

# CHAPTER FIVE

HAVING spent a sleepless Saturday night, Taryn had accepted by Sunday morning that her brief sojourn into the Nash Corporation was over. It upset her—she did not want to leave. She loved the job. Most times she loved working for the clear-minded and concise head of the company. But she knew without having to ask that he wanted one hundred per cent loyalty, and would have no time for anyone at her senior level—albeit only temporary—who did a little moonlighting on the side.

There was friction in the kitchen between her stepmother and their new housekeeper. Taryn was glad to spend hours in the study, typing back the notes she had taken in Italy on Friday.

She knew in advance that she had worked her last day for Jake, but it was a matter of pride that she completed the work before she left.

Taryn was up extra early on Monday. Were it not for the contents of her briefcase and the fact she had to return the laptop she would not have gone into the office at all. But since those papers, notes and laptop had to be delivered, she would rather go in early and receive her dismissal before anyone else was around.

Jake, always at his desk long before either she or Kate arrived, had usually made considerable inroads into his day's work before they got there.

Taryn dressed carefully in a smart two-piece of a gorgeous blue, knowing that it suited her. She needed to feel she was looking her best. She was in her office, laptop back in its usual place, at eight-fifteen.

Her insides felt as if they belonged to anyone but her when, taking a deep breath, she squared her shoulders, tapped briefly on the communicating door between the two offices, and went in.

As she had hoped, Jake was already busy at work. He looked up, pen in hand, and unsmilingly surveyed her. Taryn did not bother to sit down—she knew she would not be staying that long.

'I know you don't want to see me, but I've brought Friday's paperwork,' she said, indicating her briefcase. 'It's all typed back and—'

'Don't I pay you enough?' he cut in curtly.

Taryn inwardly sighed. It wasn't going to be straight in *You're fired* and out again, then! He clearly had plans to give her a 'talking to'.

'It isn't the money,' she answered stiffly.

'You have fantasies about the uniform?'

Sarcastic devil! 'I—was doing someone a favour,' she managed.

'I'm quite well aware of that,' he rapped, and, while she stared at him in astonishment—how could he possibly have known?— 'Sit down,' he barked, laying down his pen and indicating her usual chair.

Taryn couldn't see the point, but she was glad to sit down. Even though she resented his sharp way of speaking to her, she was shakily glad to feel the chair beneath her.

'How? How are you aware? You can't possibly—'

'Are you arguing with me?' he questioned hostilely.

Taryn tilted her chin. 'I've never been dismissed before—I'm not sure how I'm supposed to behave,' she replied woodenly, returning his hostility.

'Who says I'm dismissing you?' he grated.

This was his way of asking her to stay? 'You're—not?' she asked slowly.

'I'll let you know when.' Which left her not knowing whether she had a job or hadn't. 'According to John Buckley, when I complimented him on his staff on Saturday, many of said staff were temporary and were supplied by a Mrs Kiteley of Just Temps.'

John Buckley? John Buckley? Got him. Hotel manager. 'Er…that was your way of finding out…?'

'Who were you doing the favour for?' he gritted. 'Mrs Kiteley or her husband—your lover?'

Taryn stared at him in amazement. 'Lover?'

'You're saying that Matthew Kiteley is not your lover?' Jake Nash questioned tautly.

She could, she supposed, have told Jake all there was to tell. That Matt was Mrs Kiteley's son, not her husband, and that Mrs Kiteley was her aunt. But by then Taryn had had enough. In the short time she had been in here Jake had been at his most cold and brutish. But, given that the odds were against him keeping her on anyway, she did not have to sit here and take this.

'That's none of your business!' she snapped, before she could hold it in.

'It is my business when you spend the whole day *in my time* yawning your head off because you've spent a *busy* weekend with him!' Jake snarled.

Yawning? About to retaliate, Taryn just then recalled how dead on her feet she had been that Monday after she had typed that report for one of her aunt's clients, and how she had only managed a couple of hours' sleep.

'I hadn't had much sleep the night before—' she began.

'I don't need to hear the sordid details!' he sliced in aggressively.

'Look here, you!' Taryn was on her feet, incensed. No job was worth this! 'For your information I was short of sleep because until the early hours of Monday morning I'd been busy typing an urgently required report. And—'

'Another temping job for the same agency, no doubt?'

'It was!' she flared. 'I don't work for the agency. Well, not usually.'

'Just when there's an emergency?' he enquired, sounding a trace more reasonable, perhaps remembering how his great-uncle had urgently required a temporary housekeeper. Although in that case the temporary job had lasted quite two months.

'Exactly.'

'Hmph! Do sit down,' he said shortly, sounding impatient.

'I was supposed to be working on the reception desk at the Irwin,' she found she was telling him as she subsided back onto her chair. 'But I was late getting there…'

'My fault, of course.'

You said it! 'And the manager's wife had taken over that job. In the emergency, I—'

'But this wasn't an emergency!' he cut in, his tone toughening again.

'How do you mean?'

'You'd got it planned before we went to Italy on Thursday.'

'No, I hadn't!' she retorted indignantly.

'You said you had a date Saturday,' he reminded her bluntly.

She'd just about had it with him. 'I lied!' she snapped.

That seemed to interest him. He leaned back in his chair and studied her warm cheeks and bristling air. 'Why?' he wanted to know.

She didn't want to answer. Then, as grey eyes held hers, 'You provoked me,' she blurted out. 'And anyway, you were out on the town. It's a point of honour that I shouldn't be thought to stay home nights.'

'Because Matthew Kiteley's wife wouldn't let him come out to play?' Jake rapped.

Taryn once more experienced that head-punching feeling. He really was asking for it! 'No!' she denied hotly.

'Because you're still pining for your lost love?'

What was he talking about? Lost love? *Who* was he talking about? Abruptly it dawned on her that he must be referring to Brian Mellor. She had told Jake that she was in love with Brian. But there was no way she was going to tell him of her staggering realisation that she had probably *never* been in love with Brian, for all she had believed so at the time.

'I…' she mumbled, feeling stumped for the moment to know how to answer.

Jake was unimpressed. 'End it!' he ordered sharply.

She wasn't with him. 'End what?'

'Your job here is a demanding one,' he stated shortly. 'Things sometimes get extremely arduous around this office. I'm not having my PA—no matter how temporary—spending evenings and weekends working elsewhere. You need to be bright eyed and bushy-tailed to work here, not dead on your feet when you come in.'

Taryn wanted to argue that she never fell down on the job, but hope was rising. Did he mean that she still had her job? He had to—didn't he?

'It—isn't that easy,' she felt honour-bound to let him know, aware that she was doing herself no favours, but honesty would out.

'Because of your—attachment—to Matthew Kiteley?' Jake questioned harshly. 'End it, Taryn.'

'It's—difficult,' she answered reluctantly, knowing that, should her wonderful aunt have another emergency, she would be hard put to it to refuse to help her out.

'What's difficult about it?' he demanded toughly. And, tough not the word for it, he well and truly laid it on the line. 'If you want to continue working here, you'll give me your word.'

'I can't!' she exclaimed wretchedly.

'Can't?' He did not recognise the word.

'It's family,' she rushed on, seeing his patience was straining at the leash.

'Family?' he echoed.

'Mrs Kiteley,' she felt forced to reveal, 'is my aunt. It's hard to say no to family,' she tried to explain. 'My aunt has been so—' she broke off, Jake was looking at her in amazement.

'Mrs Kiteley of Just Temps is your *aunt?*' he doublechecked.

'Yes. She—' Taryn broke off again, a little amazed herself to see a hint of a smile tugging at the corners of Jake's superb mouth.

'Would I then be right in thinking that Matthew Kiteley, the *married* Matthew Kiteley, is your aunt's son?' he enquired silkily.

'You—um—would,' Taryn answered, trying to keep on the same track as him, but having to wonder what track he was on now.

'Matthew Kiteley is, in fact, your cousin?'

'Yes,' Taryn replied truthfully. 'Though I've always thought of Matt as more of a super big brother than my cousin.'

Jake nodded at that, but had not done with his questions yet. 'And your date with him a week ago? You may remember it—it was the night I came in and found you wandering around stark naked.'

Had he intended to make her blush, he'd quite easily succeeded. Taryn felt hot colour scorch her cheeks and hurriedly explained— anything to get him away from that subject. 'It wasn't a *date*-date. While Matt is hoping to get back together with his wife, they are separated at the moment. In the absence of his wife, I partnered him at his firm's annual dinner-dance.' She came to an end and waited, while Jake just sat and looked at her.

Then finally, his tone much softer than it had been, 'What am I going to do with you, Taryn Webster?' he asked.

'I haven't been really, really bad,' she answered.

And, to her astonishment, he burst out laughing. And Taryn found that inside she was chuckling too—from the sheer pleasure of seeing him laugh. 'I'll draw a veil over the fact you would cheerfully have let me believe you have affairs right, left and centre,' Jake remarked. But, his look alert considering and thoughtful suddenly, 'When it could well be,' he observed shrewdly, 'that the very opposite is true.'

There was no answer to that—but he seemed to be waiting for a reply. 'Um—you're getting too close,' she murmured.

'Too close to the real truth?' he took up, and, in the same breath, 'Had many lovers, Taryn?' he asked.

Crumbs! She wanted to tell him. Felt her heartbeats thundering—he was looking at her all sort of warm, pleasant... 'I meant—er—you are getting too close to—um—my private life, and...'

'I take your point,' Jake all at once agreed. 'I'm getting too personal—you wouldn't dream of asking me the same question.'

'I wouldn't dare,' she returned, and although thinking of the many legions of women he must have been to bed with was something she did not wish to dwell on, she just could not suppress a laugh of her own. She sobered when she saw the way his eyes left her eyes to go to her laughing mouth. Suddenly she was feeling all shaky inside. And, while knowing that feeling had nothing to do with why she was sitting there, 'Am I going to be allowed to stay on?' she asked quietly.

'What's a man to do when you ask so prettily?'

'Is that a yes?' she asked, and suddenly he was back to being her busy employer.

'Bring your notepad in in ten minutes,' he replied, and picked up his pen.

Taryn was so happy she was almost bursting with it as she made her way back to her own office. She was staying, and Jake, knowing all there was to know now, had not insisted that she give him her word she would not work for her aunt should another emergency arise.

Kate was happy too when she came in. 'Two mornings in a row when I haven't had to make a dive for the bathroom,' she confided. 'Fingers crossed, I'm through the rough patch.'

Strangely that day, though, Taryn experienced more shaky and fluttery sensations whenever Jake came to stand by her desk. And once, when she went in to see him with a paper that required his signature, and she waited while he first read it through, something happened to her heartstrings when she looked down at his bent head.

She drove home that night refusing to believe that her heart was involved in any way, shape or form. She determined that most definitely she was not, not, *not*, going to make a habit of falling for the men she worked for.

And yet, as she lay in her bed that night, with thoughts of Jake for no reason dominating her head, Taryn had to acknowledge that the tender feelings she had nursed for Brian Mellor in no way compared to the onslaught of feeling that Jake Nash could arouse in her.

He could make her furious, make her smile, make her want to hit him and make her want to laugh. She had felt pretty much devastated at the thought that she would that day cease working for the Nash Corporation and the career she did not wish to be parted from. Or had the thought of never, ever seeing Jake again been the real cause for her feeling so upset?

When she got up the next morning Taryn decided not to give the matter any more thought. But Jake was out of the office for most of the day—and there was no buzz about the place.

Kate continued to flourish throughout that week. And, though she was still afraid to believe she had reached the end of that awful sickness and the debilitating effects starting with a baby was having on her, she was on top form. Between them they just ate up the work. Though at Jake's insistence Kate still went home early most nights.

'Doing anything you shouldn't this weekend?' he queried to Taryn as she tidied her desk prior to leaving on Friday evening. The door between the two offices was open.

'You mean—moonlighting?' she asked, feeling sensitive on the issue.

'I'm sure you'd tell me if you were,' he answered smoothly.

'Well, I'm not. That is, I've nothing planned except to have another try at finding myself somewhere else to live.'

'You're still living with your wicked stepmother?' he asked, leaving his desk to stroll into her office.

'And my lovely father. And she's not so wicked,' she felt she had to defend. 'And things are much better since our dragon of a new housekeeper arrived...'

'They make good sparring partners, do they?'

'Like you wouldn't believe,' Taryn answered, having recently realised that her stepmother must have accepted that if she let Mrs Ferris go she was unlikely to find anyone else. But just then Taryn had other things on her mind. Not once this week had Jake asked her to dial the Almora, the Raven, or anywhere else. 'What about you?' she asked, the question refusing to stay down. 'Are you doing anything you shouldn't this weekend?'

For a moment, even though he had asked her the same question, she wondered if she had overstepped the employer-employee mark. But, no, he gave her a quite devastating smile and, as her heart-beats picked up a ridiculous speed, that smile became a grin. 'You don't really want to know the answer to that, do you?' he asked.

No, in actual fact she did not. He was obviously up to some-thing wicked, and as little darts of green picked at her Taryn very definitely did not want to know. 'Perhaps it would be better if you spared my blushes,' she said lightly—and got out of there.

On Saturday she followed up two possible apartments to let. Neither proved suitable. She tried to see potential in the smaller of the two, but it was so poky she could imagine that even her father, with his mind usually elsewhere, would look askance that she wanted to leave her spacious home to live in a rabbit hutch. The other, though much larger, went with a rent that even with her high salary made her eyes water.

She had a chat with Matt on the telephone on Sunday. He was putting a brave face on it, but because she knew him so well she knew he was down. Alison had initiated divorce proceedings.

All in all it had been a glum weekend. But as she entered the portals of the Nash Corporation, so Taryn's spirits began to lift. Perhaps she had been branded with the work ethic on the day she had been born? she mused. She certainly looked forward to the day in front of her.

Kate continued to maintain her new found good health, and

indeed started to blossom. Taryn would occasionally catch a glimpse of a more rounded tummy, but Kate somehow managed to be behind her desk when anyone other than Taryn or Jake were in her office.

It was Kate whom Jake called in late that afternoon. 'Anything I can help you with?' Taryn asked when Kate, notepad in hand came out. The time was going on if Kate wanted her work typed back before she went home.

'It will keep until tomorrow,' Kate replied. 'I'm off now— unless you need me for anything?'

It was four o'clock. Kate, it seemed was leaving extra early that day. Taryn shook her head. 'Nothing I can't handle,' she assured her, and watched her leave, reflecting how very much she would miss Kate when she went off to have her baby. How very much, too, she would miss this job, miss working in this environment, miss working for Jake, when Kate returned and she had to leave.

Still, she did not have to think about that now. Did not *want* to think about it now. Such thoughts were—painful…! Painful? She looked up, Jake had come into her office.

Unspeaking, he stood there looking down at her. She looked up at him and as she looked into his superb grey eyes, and her heart-beats thundered, she suddenly knew why to think of leaving was so painful. She—was in love with Jake Nash! Oh, my…

'You—um—wanted something?' she asked huskily, desperately trying to get herself together. It couldn't be. It *couldn't* be! It felt nothing at all like that long, long, overdrawn infatuation she had felt for Brian Mellor!

'On top of everything?' he enquired and, every bit as if he had come in to see her for a chat—a thing he had never done before—he pulled up a chair and as she half turned from her desk sat facing her.

'What…?' she began. He just didn't have time to sit and chat! But this, whatever it was, had to be work chat, not socialising chat.

'Did you find the flat you were looking for?' he asked.

Kind of him to ask! 'I've looked at a couple. Neither was suitable,' she replied, feeling wary suddenly, but with no idea why she should feel that way.

'Hmm,' he murmured, and mentioned, 'I've just asked Kate if she can cope without you.'

Alarm and something akin to panic shot through Taryn. 'You *are* getting rid of me!' she exclaimed. She had thought he would a week ago, but that crisis seemed to have passed.

'No, not at all,' he quickly assured her. 'I just wondered how you might like to have a week off?'

'I wouldn't!' she said bluntly. 'Strange as it may seem, I like it here.' He smiled that spine-melting smile—and again she was having to get herself together. 'That—a week off—is the sugar,' she accused suspiciously, and questioned, 'What's the actual pill?'

Jake stayed looking at her, his expression bland. 'I'm in a position here to be able to do you something of a favour,' he stated after a few moments.

'Given that I'm not in the habit of accepting favours from gentlemen,' she answered levelly, 'why have I this feeling that there's an ulterior motive here somewhere?'

He smiled again; it became a grin—and Taryn was ready to do whatever he asked, including jumping into the Thames fully clothed should he so wish. 'So—I'll come clean,' he said, and revealed, 'I had a telephone call from my sister last night.'

'I didn't know you had a sister.'

'I didn't know you had a cousin,' he bounced back at her, and, otherwise ignoring her interruption, continued, 'What Suzanne said started me thinking.' Taryn was silent this time. 'Suzanne and her husband, and his daughter, are booked to go on holiday on Wednesday—returning the following Tuesday.' Again Taryn said not a word, though admitted to being quite thrilled that Jake was telling her about his family. 'Anyhow, Abby—Suzanne's step-daughter—has at this late stage flatly refused to go with them.'

'How old is she?' Taryn enquired, thinking if it was just a whim the child might be coaxed out of it.

'Seventeen last week—going on thirty,' Jake answered. 'The thing is, Suzanne's husband, Stuart, is an overworked consultant surgeon who, according to my sister, desperately needs a break—no matter how short, no matter how brief.'

'Ah!' Taryn thought she saw a glimmer of light. 'But your sister's husband won't take a holiday and leave his daughter behind?'

'He has very firm views on parental responsibility. Not to mention the wild party Abby threw when they did leave her over-night not so long back. So now my sister can see the whole idea of the holiday going up in smoke unless she can find somewhere for her to stay, and with someone she knows Stuart would trust.'

'You're not suggesting that she comes and stays with me for a week!' Taryn exclaimed, realising as she did so that if she wasn't being dismissed, and yet Jake wanted her to have a week off, then he must be suggesting exactly that.

But—wrong! Already Jake was shaking his head. 'While Stuart might agree to that after he'd met you, Abby has stated that if she can't stay home by herself, the only person she will stay with—is me.'

'Even though she knows that her father is next door to being exhausted?'

'She's seventeen, and spoiled—what else can I tell you?'

'So your sister asked you to have her—Abby?' Taryn questioned, puzzling it out as she went along. 'She's stayed with you before?'

'For one night only, six months ago—it was a nightmare!'

He seemed a touch embarrassed, and Taryn suddenly caught on. 'Poor you,' she murmured, but couldn't help smiling. 'She's got a crush on you, hasn't she? This Abby, she thinks you're the best thing since waterproof mascara—and you're running scared!'

'Shut up,' he grunted, and he *was* embarrassed, Taryn could tell. Never had she thought she would ever see the day when Jake Nash would be embarrassed by anything. But having to admit that this seventeen-year-old had a crush on him was making him feel awkward. 'Anyhow, I said no—at first. I didn't like the idea one bit. I told Suzanne that I wasn't taking Abby, and explained why—she already knew anyway, about the crush thing,' he said, and went quickly on, 'I told her that I was sorry, but while I might be able to put up with her for one night, the idea of having the seventeen-year-old under my roof for six nights, just her and me, was most decidedly not going to happen.'

'Your sister wasn't very happy about that?'

'Suzanne was getting rather desperate by this time, and I was feeling the meanest brother ever born, when my sister asked couldn't I get a girlfriend to come and stay while Abby was with me.' Taryn felt a lurch in her stomach. No! she wanted to scream, as feelings of jealousy racked her. 'I said no way, but my sister can be very persuasive.' Again Taryn's stomach lurched. 'And then Suzanne pointed out that it wouldn't be a permanent move-in. And that,' he said, 'gave me an idea.'

By that time there was a green mist clouding Taryn's thinking. Otherwise she might have been more alert to where this was leading. But she wasn't, and walked straight in to enquire, 'What idea was that?'

'Now who, I asked myself, do I know who has the ability to do any kind of temporary job?'

Click. The penny dropped. 'Oh, no!' Taryn backed away fast.

'Who do I know,' he went on as if she had not spoken 'who is looking for alternative accommodation?'

'No!' Taryn said firmly, her heartbeats racing. It had to be no. Because she so wanted to say yes. So wanted to be near him in his home. 'This is the favour you said you could do me?' she asked when, having so to speak stated his case, Jake gave her space to let it sink in. 'I want a career,' she protested. 'But not in childminding!'

Jake studied her silently for long seconds. Then, 'You'll have your career, I promise,' he told her solemnly. 'Just help me out here.'

She was weakening. Taryn knew she was. 'Why can't you just tell your sister a straight no?' She stayed strong just a little longer.

'The way you told your aunt no?' he queried.

And that well and truly stumped her. Taryn stared at him. She had given in to her aunt because of the love she had for her. And it appeared Jake too could be got at by family emotions. He seemed to her, oddly, not weaker because of it, but stronger. She had witnessed a sensitivity in him—usually well hidden—before.

'If I do come to your place, I can still come here to work.' She tried to bargain anyway, but he was already shaking his head.

'If I do say yes to Suzanne, she knows it will be a one hundred per cent commitment.'

'You're going to stay home with—?'

'No,' he cut in. 'You are. Abby has a very good brain, but on occasions very little sense. Lord knows what she'll get up to let loose on her own.'

'You'd trust me to—'

'Oh, I trust you, Miss Webster,' he cut in again. 'Given that, when provoked and to save your pride, you're not averse to telling lies, I've worked with you long enough now to know I can trust you implicitly.'

She all but melted on the spot. 'Um…' She strove to keep her head. 'What about Kate? I'm supposed to be here to help her…'

'I've had a word with Kate. She said that between you you're so up to date you're in danger of meeting yourselves coming back. But should she get overloaded she has promised she will farm out any non-confidential matter.'

Taryn knew then that she had run out of arguments. And, with her heart hammering within her, she knew she was going to give in. The idea of spending a week in his home was one she was warming to by the second.

'So, let me get this straight,' she said, sobering at the thought that, while she might see him at home, she would miss seeing him during the day. Though there was the weekend… 'You want me to move into your home—er—Wednesday morning…?'

'Tuesday evening would be good. I'm not sure what time they will drop Abby off on Wednesday. I want you to be established there by the time Abby arrives.

Oh, mother! 'And I'm to act as a sort of chaperon?'

'Girlfriend,' he corrected. 'I want you to pretend to be my girlfriend.'

*Oh, mother* didn't cover it. Taryn swallowed—only just then an unexpected imp of mischief came and tripped her up. 'Er—I take it you're going to be true to me—for a week?' she murmured, her eyes big and beautiful. And she loved it when he laughed.

'Oh, Taryn Webster, there's more to you than meets the eye, isn't there?' He sobered as he went on, 'I promise to eat home every night.' He went further, 'And to give you my undivided attention.'

'There's no need to go totally overboard!' she told him. But suddenly they were both laughing. Oh, my word, how she loved him.

Taryn went home that night with her head in a whirl. She was head over heels in love with Jake, and starting tomorrow she was going to live with him in his home for a whole week!

She had no idea how this feeling of love for him had come about. She didn't think she had even liked him very much at the start—though, feeling as she did now, she could not quite remember how she had felt then. For it seemed to her now that she had always loved Jake—and it was nothing at all like those feelings she had nursed for so long over Brian Mellor. Her deep regard for Brian, she saw now, had been because he was a good and kind man. But it had never been love. Even before that one lapse, when he had fallen off the pedestal she had put him on, she had never felt for him this all consuming emotion she felt for Jake. She loved Jake, was in love with Jake. Jake was in her head from morning till night in a way that Brian had never been.

Taryn packed a large suitcase ready to stow in her car the next morning. She hoped she had packed everything she would need, but, since it would take her less than an hour to come back for anything else she might need, she was not too concerned.

Her stepmother, having at present called a truce with Mrs Ferris, had no comment to make when Taryn told her and her father that she was going to stay with a friend for a week.

Her father brought his mind temporarily away from problem solving to enquire, 'One of your college friends?'

Taryn was unable to lie to her father. 'I'm staying with Jake,' she owned, while wondering if he would remember who Jake was. 'He has company staying. I'm…'

'Making up the numbers, eh?' he said with a smile, and, not waiting for an answer, 'So long as you're happy, love.'

Taryn left her suitcase in the boot of her car and went into the office with her stomach churning. If she had got it right, there would be just her and Jake at his home that night.

She felt pretty much churned up all day, and, love Jake though she did, she started to have second thoughts about the wisdom of what she was doing. She saw him most every day at his office. But with a door more often than not closed between them, not to mention that at the office it was business, business, business all the way, it would have been no trouble to hide her feelings for him. And keep them well hidden she must. But would it be so easy at home? Living at his home? Pride reared up—it was jolly well going to have to be.

'See you in a week's time,' Kate said, when at ten to five she started tidying her desk.

'I'll look forward to it,' Taryn answered.

'You'll be all right,' Kate assured her cheerfully. 'How much trouble can a seventeen-year-old cause?'

It was not the seventeen-year-old Taryn was worried about.

With their work up to date, she set about clearing her own desk shortly after Kate had gone home.

And it was around five-fifteen that the door between the two offices opened and Jake strolled through. 'Ready for home?' he asked, his manner easy.

'When you are,' she replied.

He accepted that with a small inclination of his head, and, putting a hand into his pocket, he took out a key. 'You'd better hang on to that.'

She supposed, should she and Abby be going out somewhere— and they couldn't stay cooped up indoors the whole time—that to have her own key was essential.

'Thank you,' she accepted—rather stiltedly, she realized. And could only love Jake the more when he seemed to notice that she was more than a degree or two uptight.

Because suddenly he stretched out a hand and with a light finger tapped her on the nose. 'Race you home,' he challenged, and she just had to laugh. He was a gentleman too, in that he let her leave the office first.

In actual fact he arrived at his home before her, but was waiting on the pavement for her, first of all to haul her case out from the boot, and then to instruct her where to park her car.

She was glad she had been to his home before, because that made it seem less strange—for all most of her time there had been spent with him in his study.

'Come upstairs,' Jake said, hefting up her case, 'and I'll show you your room.'

It was a lovely room, large and airy, like the one she had at home. A touch austere, perhaps, but this was a male residence so Taryn had not expected pastels.

'Very nice,' she murmured politely.

'I'll leave you to unpack. Mrs Vincent comes in for a couple of hours most days. She was going to concoct some sort of a salad,' he commented. 'Come down when you're ready,' he tacked on easily, and left her to it.

With there being nothing to spoil about a salad if it was left waiting, Taryn investigated the adjoining bathroom, unpacked, and decided to take a shower.

After which she donned lightweight trousers and a loose top and, her hair having been pulled back in a knot all day, she left it loose and went downstairs.

She found Jake in the drawing room, reading his evening paper. 'Don't get up,' she said. Too late—he was already on his feet. 'I thought I'd investigate the kitchen,' she suggested. 'You know— familiarise myself with the layout.'

'You're being very good about this,' Jake complimented. Her heart sang. *Race you home,* he had said. Incredibly, it was already starting to feel like home. She would have to watch that.

'I like to do my job properly,' she said primly, just to let him know—and to more firmly remind herself—that this was a job to her and nothing more.

They had stepped several paces towards each other by this time. She halted when they were a couple of yards distant. But as she looked at him so Jake, a more giving look about him than was noticeable at the office, studied her. His glance flicked to her long blonde hair, to her eyes, to her mouth, and back up to her eyes again. Then he smiled. 'Feel free to wander around where you please,' he invited.

They had dinner just after seven. Mrs Vincent had prepared a superb cold soufflé starter. There was a ham salad to follow, and raspberries and ice cream to finish off with. Taryn had thought that any conversation they had was bound to be work-related. But not a bit of it.

'You live at home with your father, stepmother and a dragon housekeeper, I believe?' Jake queried at the start of their meal.

She had pretty much told him that bit, Taryn recalled, but she was pleased that he had not brought her into his home to then just ignore her.

'Mrs Ferris, the housekeeper, isn't so bad once you get to know her. In fact,' Taryn confided, 'I quite like her.'

'Bet you haven't told your stepmother that!'

Taryn had to laugh. 'She's not so bad either,' she said.

'You told your father you were coming here for a week?' Jake asked.

'This soufflé is delicious. I'll have to ask your Mrs Vincent for the recipe.'

'What did he say?'

There was no avoiding the question. 'I couldn't lie outright to my father, Jake,' she told him solemnly, and was pleased to see his expression stayed pleasant.

'I wouldn't expect you to,' he answered.

Taryn breathed an inward sigh of relief. Jake was a very private person. She knew he would not want his business, work and personal life broadcast. 'I told him I was staying with Jake who had company staying,' she revealed. 'From that my father gathered there would be a few of us here, and wished me happy.'

'You're close to him?'

Taryn wasn't quite sure how to answer that. 'I feel close to him a lot of the time. He—well, he's a sort of retired experimental scientist. Only it seems impossible for his non-retired brain to stop delving into matters scientific and experimental.' She smiled. 'Sometimes the dear love is the only one on his particular planet.'

'His head's in another world?'

That just about summed him up, Taryn had to agree. 'More often than not,' she replied.

'Was that why your mother went to Africa?'

'She met someone who noticed she was there.'

'You miss her?'

This was getting a bit personal, a bit emotionally personal. But Taryn loved him. And, although she was a private person too, she found she was answering. 'Yes, I miss her. But she's happy with her new husband, with her new life—and…' Taryn smiled, and to lighten the mood explained. 'And I have my Aunt Hilary to give me a hug should I have a down moment.'

By then they were eating the ham salad. 'Do you get many of those? Down moments?' Jake asked.

She shook her head. 'It was a bit bewildering at the time,' she commented and, having said that much, found she was going on, 'I was fifteen, and torn between wanting to help my father—who seemed quite baffled as to why my mother was leaving him—and wondering what I could do, or should have done, to make my mother want to stay. But Aunt Hilary was always there—and now I'm over it,' Taryn ended brightly. And, thinking that was more than enough to have revealed, she searched around for a question she could ask him that was not connected with work, but which was not too personal either.

But before she could get started Jake was delving too deeply into 'personal' when, seated opposite her, his eyes on her eyes, he enquired politely, 'What happened between you and Brian Mellor?'

Her mouth fell open. She wasn't going to answer. Of course Jake did not know just how personal his question was—even if she had told him that she loved Brian. 'I told you,' she answered, a cool note entering her tones.

'No, you didn't,' Jake denied, entirely unperturbed by her cool tone. 'I know you walked out on him. But you never said why.'

'I—did,' she muttered.

'You said you fell in love with him. But that hadn't happened overnight. Presumably you'd loved him for some while—so what happened to make you so upset you were next door to tears when you got into the lift that day?'

'You're—getting too personal!' she stated bluntly.

He was not the smallest bit put off. 'What could be more personal than you telling me you were in love with him?'

'You made me cross. I wouldn't have mentioned it otherwise!'

she erupted. Honestly! Some things were sacred. She had answered all his other questions, perhaps because she could see their relevance should his step-niece start asking questions to which a close boyfriend would be likely to know the answers. But *really*—there were limits.

'He—Mellor—he obviously loved you,' Jake commented, ignoring her frosty look.

'No, he didn't!' Taryn exploded, and could have thumped Jake Nash when one of his eyebrows went aloft.

'Curiouser and curiouser,' he quoted. 'Was that why you left in a fit of pique—because he didn't love you?'

'No, I didn't!' she exclaimed angrily, adding unthinkingly, 'If you must know, he kissed me.' She glared at him with storming blue eyes. Urgh! This man!

Jake looked back, totally unmoved. 'He kissed you?' he repeated, his eyes missing nothing of her flashing eyes. 'He'd kissed you before, though?' he remarked.

'No, he hadn't!'

'Not so much as a peck on the cheek?'

'Nothing that personal at all!' she seethed.

Jake gave a small shrug. 'So on the day he did decide to give you a little peck, it all became...'

'It wasn't just a little peck!' she flared.

'Ah! He really meant business,' Jake let fall mockingly.

Taryn tossed him an incensed look. But, having revealed far more than she had ever meant to, she suddenly wanted it all said and over. 'If you must know, it was a—a lover's kiss,' she hissed.

'Mmm!' Jake murmured. 'You responded?'

What was it with this man? 'No, I didn't!' she replied heatedly. Though, as her innate honesty came and tripped her up, 'I—think I wanted to, but I didn't.'

'You didn't?'

'I was afraid I might.'

'That's why you bolted? You were afraid you might give in, and got out of there because you're a "good girl" and didn't want to play that game?'

Jake Nash, with his mocking talk of 'good girl', was infuriating. 'He didn't want to play any game!' she snapped frostily, and felt her Jake Nash thumping tendencies return when his look became sceptical.

'Just how much do you know about men?' he enquired forthrightly.

And she wasn't having that. She might no longer love Brian, but she still believed him good, kind, and not the sort of man who would be interested in an affair outside of his marriage. 'It might not have dawned on me at the time,' she erupted, 'but I've since realised that Brian was probably only half aware that it was me he was holding.'

'He's in the habit of grabbing hold of just about anyone, is he?'

Taryn ignored his sarcasm, but was still defending her ex-employer's actions as, less heatedly, she explained, 'I think he and his wife were having a few problems. He just—sort of needed someone to—er… Oh, I don't know. Hold on to—hug, I suppose. Someone to hug him back. I feel sure now that it was Angie, his wife, that he wanted to kiss…'

'Only she was off him?'

Taryn sighed. 'Something like that, I suppose.'

'So he kissed you, and you, with your little puritan heart, were shocked to feel a—wanting man—so up close. Shocked to think you might weaken and respond—so you did the only thing possible: you hurtled out of there.'

She had had enough. She could do without the raspberries and ice cream. She stood up. 'If you've finished, I'll get these dishes washed.'

Jake, plainly not interested in raspberries and ice cream either, got to his feet, surveyed her warring expression and decided against whatever it was he had been about to say. 'Are you too angry to let me help?' he enquired charmingly—and all of a sudden, totally unexpectedly, Taryn wanted to laugh.

She restrained it, and managed to keep her voice quite waspish when she snapped, 'You don't get away with it that easily.'

As it happened there was a dishwasher of the same make as the one they had in her home. Taryn's equilibrium was almost fully restored by the time the kitchen was neat and tidy once more. But she had had sufficient of Jake's probing questions for one night, and, love him though she did, she decided to make herself scarce.

'I think I'll go up,' she said, and even managed a hint of a smile.

'It might be an idea if you had a look around upstairs,' Jake replied. But, as if aware that she was unlikely to go poking into the various upstairs rooms, 'I'll come up with you,' he offered.

Upstairs he matter-of-factly showed her the room that was already made up for his step-niece, the large linen cupboard, and a couple of other rooms. Then he walked back along the landing with her.

'Goodnight,' she bade him as she halted at the door of her room.

'You'd better take a look in my room,' Jake remarked, his manner again matter-of-fact.

'Oh, I don't think that's necessary,' she stated in a rush, feeling awkward suddenly.

'You don't?' Jake enquired, grey eyes steadily looking down at her. 'I did make it clear you're supposed to be my live-in girlfriend?'

'I'm not sleeping with you!' Taryn flew, before she could hold the words in.

And that caused Jake to rock back on his heels and stare at her. 'Don't look so alarmed,' he advised, a mocking light coming to his eyes. 'You might enjoy it.'

'Look here, you…' she began, only couldn't finish because suddenly he was looking highly amused.

'Oh, little Taryn Webster,' he said softly, of her five feet nine. 'Given that I haven't asked that of you, I doubt I'd fare any better than any other man.'

'What do you mean by that?' she demanded, though rather thought she knew.

'From my observations, and hard to believe though I find it, I'd say—beautiful as you undoubtedly are—that no man has ever persuaded you to say yes.'

What he was saying, Taryn realized, looking quickly away from him, was that somehow or other—and heaven alone knew how, because she wasn't wearing a label—Jake Nash knew that she was a virgin.

She opened her mouth, wanting to say something—something witty, something bright. But all she could come up with was a husky, 'What you never have you never miss.' She dared a look at him—and saw that the mocking light had gone, and had been replaced by a look that was almost—tender!

'Oh, Taryn!' he said softly. But then seemed to gather himself together. 'Goodnight,' he said abruptly, and stood back so she should go into her room.

Taryn did not hang about. She had already said goodnight. Without a word, having not seen inside his room, she went into her room and closed the door.

# CHAPTER SIX

To HER surprise, Taryn had the best night's sleep she'd had in ages. She awoke bright-eyed and clear-headed, and realised that Jake was right. If they were to make his seventeen-year-old step-niece believe that they were living together in the accepted sense, then Abby—a clever Abby, from the little Jake had told her—would not be fooled in the slightest if said live-in girlfriend hadn't a clue what the inside of his bedroom looked like.

Taryn got out of bed, listened, but heard not a sound. She glanced at her watch—just gone seven. Had Jake already left for his office? He was always there before her and Kate, so he was very probably continuing with his habitual early start.

She showered and dressed, hoping that Jake had some idea of what time Abby would be arriving, and hoping too that he intended taking an hour off work to be here when his guest arrived.

Taryn left her room and, not having heard a sound, was convinced that if Jake was not already in his office, he must be on his way there. She was at the head of the stairs when suddenly she halted. This was ridiculous! For the sake of authenticity Jake had deemed it a good idea that she know what the inside of his bedroom looked like. Though why he could not just explain that she was a platonic friend he had staying with him, she could not imagine. Though, on second thoughts, recalling the handsome virile look of him, would any bright seventeen-year-old believe that?

Probably not. Most very probably not, Taryn decided and, instead of going down the stairs, went along the landing to the only room she had not looked in on.

Still fully believing that Jake was out of the house, she turned the door handle and went in. His room, though larger, was pretty much the same as hers, she saw. Although apart from the usual bedroom furniture he also had a desk and the inevitable computer.

His bed was unmade. She went over to it and stripped back the covers and, taking hold of the pillow where he had laid his head, felt close to him.

In actual fact she was closer than she had foreseen because, halfway through making his bed, and when she had not heard a sound all morning, suddenly a movement behind her had the hairs on the back of her neck standing on end.

Spinning round, she went crimson. Her mouth fell open, but no sound came. Jake, however, was not similarly transfixed. Even while standing there, naked with the exception of a towel around his middle, he managed to sound casual as he greeted her. 'Good morning, Taryn. Sleep well?' he enquired.

Her eyes were riveted on his broad, manly chest, with its traces of dark damp hair, and her blush deepened as she raised her eyes to his.

'You said... I... Sorry,' she stumbled. 'I thought I'd better check your room.'

'There's no need for you to make my bed,' he answered smoothly, fully aware of her blushing countenance, her feeling of discomfort, while he, his long legs showing beneath the short towel around his middle, appeared not the least embarrassed or put out.

'I'll—um—go,' she said in a rush, knowing that she was going to have to move closer to him to skirt around him. But he was blocking her way. 'I—thought you'd gone to the office,' she mumbled as she took a few paces nearer.

'Somehow I guessed you did,' he answered, and, seeing a glint of wickedness in his superb grey eyes, Taryn lowered her gaze. But she could not help but wonder if he was laughing at her.

She was by then close up to him—he still hadn't moved out of her way. 'Excuse me,' she requested politely.

'Of course.' He did not move an inch.

She was getting annoyed—or was it nerves getting to her? She hadn't time to analyse which. 'You're a bit—um—n-naked,' she rephrased her *excuse me*, trying not to look at his uncovered nipples which, for no reason, she was finding quite fascinating.

'True,' he replied suavely. 'But I hope not too worrying for you.'

She looked up then, straight up and into his eyes, and had the awful feeling that he knew everything that was going on in her head. She swallowed. 'Not at all,' she replied, as nonchalantly as she was able.

His glance on her was warm, friendly, even understanding. Then he seemed to collect himself and stepped out of her way. 'Give me five minutes,' he said, 'and I'll join you downstairs.'

Taryn did not hang about, but got out of there on winged feet. She should have checked his bathroom first. No, that wasn't right. That would have been even worse. She might have caught him entirely towel-less then!

Five minutes wasn't long enough for her to get herself back together again. Which was why she was glad that Jake left it ten minutes before he, fully dressed, joined her downstairs.

'This isn't going to work,' she said in a rush, as soon as she saw him.

'Yes, it is,' he answered smoothly. 'That was just a small blip. But, since I have this feeling that you're going to make trebly sure it doesn't happen again—' he was right there—make it quadruply sure— 'why don't we sit down and have a nice cup of tea?'

'Dutch uncle!' she retorted, but had to laugh when he

laughed, having cottoned on that he *was* speaking to her like some Dutch uncle—though where that expression had come from she hadn't a clue.

Over tea and toast Jake explained that his sister and brother-in-law would be dropping Abby off any time soon, on their way to the airport. And that Mrs Vincent, his daily, would arrive around nine.

'Won't Abby think it odd that I don't know your part-time house-keeper? Presumably you'll be off to your office as soon as you can?'

'You'll handle it,' Jake responded confidently. Taryn wished she had his confidence.

But she took to his sister straight away when, with Abby in tow, Suzanne and her husband arrived. Although it was Abby who bounded in first, the moment Jake opened the door to them.

'*Jake!*' Her squeal of delight reached Taryn, who was waiting in the drawing room.

There followed a murmur of voices, of greetings, then she heard Jake say, 'Come and say hello to Taryn.'

'Taryn?' Abby exclaimed; clearly her stepmother had forgotten to impart the news that Jake already had company.

Any idea Taryn might have at first nursed that Abigail Braithwaite was a child vanished the moment she clapped eyes on her. Jeans-and-top-clad—a very *low* top, with a cleavage to knock the eye out—Abby preceded the others into the room.

Taryn smiled at her. Abby did not return her smile. Then Jake was there, making the introductions, and Suzanne was making up for her step-daughter's coldness by greeting her warmly. Stuart Braithwaite greeted her cheerfully too. Taryn looked into his tired eyes and considered that a month away would do him the world of good—but it had taken all of Suzanne's persuasions to get him to take a week off, apparently.

'We'll have to dash,' he said, refusing her offer of coffee. 'It took us longer to get here than I thought. And you know these airlines—they want you there before the pilot has left his bed.'

'I'll take your case up to your room,' Jake told Abby once her father and stepmother had gone.

'Is it the same one as last time?'

'Taryn has that one,' Jake replied.

'Taryn *lives* here?' Abby questioned sourly, flicking an unsmiling look in Taryn's direction.

'I knew you wouldn't mind,' he said teasingly, hefting up her over-large case.

'Why does she need her own bedroom?' Abby wanted to know, not backward in asking for answers to that which she did not know.

'One of us snores,' he answered lightly, and Abby trailed after him up the stairs.

She came down the stairs with him too, chattering away, only to clam up the moment she saw her step-uncle's 'girlfriend'.

Taryn guessed she was in for a fun day, and when Jake said that he would 'get off now' she quite desperately wanted to go to the office too. Grief—a week of this!

'All right, Taryn?' he asked, coming over to her.

'Fine.' She forced a smile.

'I'll try and get home early,' he murmured, up close, she supposed making it seem as if he was saying an affectionate goodbye. 'Be good.' He smiled—and all but turned her legs to water when he slipped an arm about her shoulders and laid his lips on hers.

'Heavens—you've got it bad!' Abby exclaimed when, Jake gone, Taryn still stood there.

Taryn forced a self-deprecating grin. 'What can I tell you?' she shrugged, and hoped that, if she had just confirmed to Abby that she was in love with Jake, should Abby happen to pass that on Jake would believe she had merely been acting out the role she had been given. 'What would you like to do today?' she asked brightly.

'I'd better go and unpack.'

Abby was still upstairs when Mrs Vincent arrived, which was

a blessing. Taryn was able to introduce herself without the intelligent Abby asking questions.

'Is Abby here yet?' Mrs Vincent asked, aware, since it was she who had made up the beds, that there were two houseguests.

'She's upstairs unpacking,' Taryn replied, realising Mrs Vincent would remember Abby from her previous visit.

'Is there anything special you would like for dinner tonight? I could make a steak pie that Mr Nash is fond of.'

'Would it be any trouble?' Taryn asked, very undecided about her role suddenly. Mrs Vincent seemed to think that she was mistress here—when in Taryn's view she had only signed up to keep Abby out of his hair.

When Abby eventually came down the stairs she had changed into a less revealing top and looked to be on her way out.

'Come and say hello to Mrs Vincent,' Taryn suggested lightly.

'Sure,' Abby replied off-handedly. But Taryn had to give her top marks for good manners when she chatted pleasantly to Mrs Vincent for a few minutes before she said she was 'off out'.

'Going anywhere special?' Taryn followed her into the hall to enquire.

Abby shrugged. 'I thought about hitting the shops,' she replied. But unbent sufficiently to ask, 'Fancy it?'

Quite honestly, no. Against that, it did not seem right to let the seventeen-year-old trail around London on her own. 'Love to,' Taryn answered. 'Hang on while I get my bag.'

Abigail Braithwaite was something of a shopping queen, Taryn very soon realized. Because it seemed to her that there were very few shops in London that they did not visit. Abby selected, tried on, discarded—and was indefatigable. At Taryn's insistence they took a break from shopping to have a snack—then it was off to the shops again. Though when they eventually returned to Jake's home Taryn could not have said Abby was very much warmer to her.

Taryn forgave her, however. Abby had one giant-sized crush on

Jake—and she was experiencing some of that same agony over him herself.

True to his word, he came home early. That was, he walked in at half past six and came straight over to Taryn. 'How's my girl?' he asked. If only! He kissed her. She liked it. Even if he had caused a riot to start clanging away inside her.

'Don't I get a kiss too?' Abby protested loudly.

'Of course,' Jake replied, adding, as he adroitly avoided the lips she offered and planted a light kiss on her cheek, 'You're precious too.' Abby glowed. 'What did you do today?' he asked.

Jake, it appeared, had eaten at lunchtime, but could not resist a helping of Mrs Vincent's steak pie with some salad. By that time both Taryn and Abby were starving, and tucked into the meal with relish—Abby keeping up a commentary on their raid of the shops.

'So what did you buy?' he enquired, keeping the conversation going.

'Well, we didn't actually buy anything, apart from bits and pieces. But I had fun trying,' Abby laughed. 'Well, I *was* enjoying it until Taryn made us stop and have something to eat,' she complained.

Jake smiled at her and turned the conversation. But later, when Abby went from the room to take a telephone call from her father, 'I've been remiss,' he said.

'I'm sure you have,' Taryn agreed. 'But—how?'

He looked at her as if he liked her. Taryn almost purred. 'I should have given you some money to—'

'No, you shouldn't!' Taryn cut in at once.

'I don't expect you to pay for Abby's meals,' he said heavily.

'You're embarrassing me!' Taryn flared.

'Again?'

He could only be referring to her seeing him next to naked that morning. She recalled his comment when *he* had been embarrassed after she'd said that Abby had a crush on him. 'Oh—shut up!' she exclaimed, regardless that he was her boss and that somehow next week she was going to have to resume an employer-employee relationship.

But it seemed that she had amused him, because he laughed at her 'shut up' and she just had to join in.

'What's the joke?' Abby wanted to know, coming into the room at that moment.

'Just Taryn making me feel good,' he replied. 'Your father all right?'

'Sounds better already,' Abby answered, and Taryn began to suspect that Abby, while at the same time feeling she had a right to be a perverse-minded seventeen-year-old, worried about her father more than she was letting on.

From there, Jake went on to ask Abby, who had decided to leave school, what plans she had for her future.

'Work, you mean?'

'It's not a dirty word,' he teased her.

'Dad said something about me staying on and going to university—doing something with one of the sciences.'

'You could,' Jake commented, without pressure. 'Your exam results are first class.'

'Who told you that?' But she had no need to ask. Both Suzanne and her father were very proud of her.

'Taryn's father is a scientist.' Jake included Taryn in the conversation, although she had been quite happy just to sit and listen to the easy way Jake spoke to his step-niece. She guessed he would have found it far more difficult had she not been there, and was suddenly glad that he had felt able to ask her to help him out with Abby.

'Is he?' Abby, her interest sparked, was looking at her.

'He's retired now. But he still has his workshops, and usually has some project or other on the go.'

Abby took that in. 'You don't work yourself, Taryn?' she asked, trying to sound nice, but it was obvious to Taryn, and no doubt to

Jake too, that if he expected women to work, then he ought to look in his girlfriend's direction first.

'I've an aunt who runs a temping agency.'

'You do temp work?'

'As a favour to me Taryn is having a week off, to keep you company,' Jake cut in. Abby didn't look too thrilled at the news.

Taryn wondered at what time they would go to bed. She was ready to go to her room now, but realised that Jake would prefer she stayed down until Abby, resplendent in another eye-poppingly low-cut top, decided to call it a day.

In the event it was Jake who was the first to move. 'If you'll excuse me? I've a few matters to deal with in my study,' he said, and left them to it.

And Abby, clearly preferring male company, decided she would go upstairs, take a bath and go to bed.

'I'll come up too,' Taryn said with a smile—and was honoured with her first smile from Abby for her pains. Apparently Abby felt better to know that she was not the only one who was deprived of Jake's company.

An hour later Taryn was sitting up in bed reading. That was to say she had a book in her hands, but was staring into space, her mind elsewhere, when her bedroom door opened and Jake strolled in.

Immediately, as her heart began to race, she became aware of her uncovered shoulders and her cotton camisole that was so fine it was next to transparent. Hastily she put down her book and bunched the bedcovers modestly up to her chin. How dear he was… 'You forgot to tell me something?' she questioned—a shade waspishly, it was true, but she felt at a decided disadvantage.

'I won't stay long,' he answered, coming over and parking himself on the side of the bed. 'Abby's floating about—I thought I'd better keep the authenticity thing going.'

'You want her to think we're—er—having a bit of a—um—cuddle?'

'It's going better than I'd hoped. But, nice kid though she otherwise is, she won't miss a thing.'

'This is getting to be much more—intimate than I realised when—'

'You're not thinking of backing out?' he bit sharply.

And Taryn burst out laughing. 'You're terrified!' she accused.

He gave a shame-faced grin. 'But for my sister, I'd sort the kid out. But I can't risk Abby getting upset and toddling off somewhere.'

'It's a hard life,' Taryn mourned, trying to stop her lips from twitching. Then she became aware of Jake's arrested kind of look on her, and her breath seemed suddenly suspended.

'You really are incredibly beautiful,' seemed to leave his lips without his own volition.

Oh, heavens. Once again her heart started hammering. 'I— er…' she tried. 'Perhaps you've been in here for long enough?' she managed.

'Oh, Taryn, I wasn't—getting fresh' Jake apologised.

She knew that, and told him so. 'I know. It's just that…'

'You're not very comfortable with me here?'

And all at once in this upside down world in which she found herself Taryn knew that she did not want Jake to go. Which made it about the oddest thing she had ever done to date that she should tell him, 'Goodnight, Jake.'

He looked at her a moment or two longer. Seemed about to lean forward as though to kiss her goodnight. But he checked, stood up, and, 'Sleep tight,' he bade her, and left.

It was only after he had gone that she realised that she had not asked him about work, about Kate. It was an upside down world true enough. Her job meant everything to her—well, almost everything.

Jake took them both out to dinner the next evening, and Taryn felt as swoony over him as Abby from the special attention he was showing her. Oh, if only it were true, and not put on for Abby's benefit.

'I need to spend an hour or so in the study,' Jake said when they returned to the house.

'I'll say goodnight,' Abby stated, and went towards the stairs.

Taryn went to follow her, only for her heart to start to go wild when Jake caught a hold of her and turned her about. 'Goodnight, my darling,' he said softly. And, while Taryn just stood and stared up at him, mesmerised, he gathered her into his arms and, holding her close up to him, kissed her.

It was not a brief wisp of a kiss, but a full-blown, mouth lingering on mouth kiss. Vaguely Taryn knew that he was only kissing her because Abby must be waiting at the bottom of the stairs for her. And that the kiss was only because Abby was there.

'G-goodnight,' Taryn said huskily, when the kiss ended.

But that was not the end. Because as Jake looked at her so his head neared hers again, and this time as his lips touched hers, so without any instruction from her, Taryn's arms went round him. And never had she known such bliss.

She felt his arms tighten about her at her response, and she forgot totally about Abby and everything else as she just clung on to him, and held on to him.

Taryn was not at all sure which one of them pulled back first. She hoped it was her. But she just didn't know. All she knew was that she loved him, and that she was in the circle of his arms, where she wanted to be.

Which made it the oddest thing ever that she should take a step back. Jake took a step back too, his arms falling to his sides. She opened her mouth, desperately seeking for something trite to say that might begin to hide what she was feeling.

Then she remembered that Abby was there watching. 'Intimate, did I say?' Taryn managed huskily, hoping Jake would think her low, husky tone was because she didn't want Abby to hear. Only then did Taryn realise that she still had her hands at his waist. She took another step back. 'I'd better let you go,' she said lightly, then realised that wasn't what she'd meant to convey, and that it sounded as if she never wanted to let him go, so hurriedly added, as pink invaded her cheeks, 'to work.' Abruptly then, before she made an even bigger fool of herself, she turned quickly around.

Abby was nowhere in sight! Taryn, without looking back, went straight up to her room. Oh, my word, this had got to stop. Jake had kissed her—oh, my, how he'd kissed her. And she wanted more. But that kiss—correction, two kisses—had not been for her benefit but because Abby—prior to getting fed up with waiting—had been there. And that, Taryn saw, made it no kiss at all—for him at any rate.

By morning she had got herself back in one piece again. By morning it was written large in her mind that Jake had not kissed her because he found her irresistible—joke—but because he had been trying to convince a watching Abby that she was wasting her time if she was still having romantic thoughts about him.

Taryn had agonised a little about facing him again, wanting to see him but feeling shy—she must stop thinking of those moments in his arms. But she need not have worried about any awkwardness because she did not see him. Instead, she came out of her shower to find he had pushed a note under her door.

'Early start,' it read. 'May be late back. Enjoy your day.' It was signed 'J'.

For all of a second she experienced a warm glow that he had stopped to write a note. Then she began to wonder that he had written at all! If he'd had any news to impart he could more easily have popped his head around her door. And, prior to kissing her last night, she felt sure he would have done just that.

She found it worrying. Had she shown her feelings for him? By responding, had she…? Taryn stopped her imaginings right there. She concentrated instead on getting through the day.

'What shall we do today?' It was Abby who, when acquainted with the fact Jake had already left for work and might be very late getting home, asked the question.

'Anything you like,' Taryn answered, pleased to see that Abby was a touch warmer to her. Perhaps she was coming to terms with the uselessness of her infatuation for Jake?

'I could go and take another look at that blue dress I tried on yesterday. We could have lunch out too, if we're having a late dinner.'

Part of Taryn enjoyed ambling around with nothing very specific to do. But a bigger part of her pulled to be hard at work in her office.

Time was going on by the time, with the blue dress in its large shiny carrier, Abby asked, 'Where do you usually go for lunch?'

To say she usually got something from the staff canteen at the Nash Corporation might be too risky, Taryn considered. Then realised that they were not too far away from the restaurant she had sometimes used when she had worked for Brian Mellor.

'I know the very place,' she said.

The New Recruit seemed as it always had. And it was very flattering that their waiter remembered her, and seemed to give them priority treatment.

After a very satisfying meal, however, they were at the door, on their way out, when they bumped into someone coming in.

'Taryn!' the man exclaimed.

She halted, Abby halting with her.

'Brian!' Taryn looked at him, startled. She had not seen Brian Mellor since the day she had walked out on him. She owned to feeling a shade awkward. It was a surprise to see him there—Brian had never used to eat there, most times preferring a sandwich at his desk and then a dinner at night, cooked by Angie. 'How are you?' she asked.

'Missing you!' he promptly stated, not needing to think about it.

'Er—how's Angie?' she asked, intending to ask after the children and then find a slot to introduce Abby.

'We're getting divorced,' he answered. Which was such a total shock that Taryn forgot entirely about introducing Abby and stared at him in amazement. He and Angie were devoted to each other!

'What are you doing now?' he asked, before she could ask him what on earth had gone wrong.

'Er…' Then it was that she remembered Abby. 'I'm doing a bit of temping,' Taryn replied.

'Come back and work for me,' Brian urged. 'I know I made an awful blunder, but you'll never know how sorry I am about that. I am sorry, Taryn. Please believe me.'

Oh, crumbs, this was getting embarrassing. 'Of course I believe you,' she said, aware of Abby standing there, looking intrigued. 'I'll—er—give you a ring,' she said, feeling helpless suddenly, but committed to telephoning him. 'Um, we're blocking the way,' she said, as a couple tried to get past. Separated from Abby for the moment, in the jumble of bodies, she decided against making the introduction, but said, 'Bye, Brian.'

'Make it soon.'

'Who was that?' Abby asked as they came away from the restaurant.

'Oh, just a man I used to work for,' Taryn answered lightly.

They returned to Jake's home, Abby taking her purchase upstairs to hang in her wardrobe.

They had cheese on toast around seven, and Jake arrived home just after eight. His eyes went straight to Taryn. She thought he looked tired, and from love for him, but knowing he would think she was playing this his way, went over to him and, stretching up, kissed him lightly on the lips.

She then realised that he was not that tired when an arm snaked out and he held her briefly, his tired eyes looking down at her. 'You make a man glad he's come home,' he said softly.

She laughed lightly. She loved him. 'Have you had anything to eat?'

'I have, but I could murder a coffee.'

'I'll have one too!' Abby piped up, clearly of the opinion she had been neglected long enough.

'Had a good day?' Jake asked her.

'I bought a dress,' she informed him.

While Jake took his briefcase into his study, Taryn went to make some coffee. It was good to have him home. She had not seen him since last night—she missed him.

Apart from the fact she had made a mental note that she was now going to have to ring Brian—she would tell him then that she had a permanent job—and apart from occasionally wondering what the Dickens had happened that had brought the Mellors to the divorce courts, Taryn had more or less forgotten bumping into Brian at lunchtime. Though the fact that he was now eating out at lunchtime seemed to endorse that Angie was no longer cooking him an evening meal.

If she had put Brian and his unhappy family circumstances from her mind, however, it soon became apparent that Abby had not. They were seated in the drawing room, drinking coffee, when, although she had not been formally introduced to him, she suddenly asked Taryn, 'What did Brian do that made him so sorry?'

Jake's head jerked up. 'Brian?' he questioned, his glance going instantly to Taryn, just those two syllables—'Brian'—sounding accusatory. 'Brian Mellor?'

'We bumped into him,' Taryn replied calmly.

'He wants Taryn to go back and work for him,' Abby piped up.

'Does he, now?' Jake still had his eyes on Taryn.

'He's getting divorced,' Abby persisted.

'Is that right?' Jake asked Taryn sharply.

'That's what he said,' she replied.

'Hmph!' Jake grunted. But, to show just how little he was bothered about that, he changed the subject completely to ask his step-niece, 'Have you spoken with your father today?'

'He rang earlier,' Abby answered. 'He's an old fusspot,' she went on, it clear to Taryn that she thought the world of her father. 'I *could* have stayed at home, you know.'

'And deprived Taryn and me of your company? We couldn't have let you do that,' Jake said charmingly.

Abby beamed at him. 'They got really mad at me when they went away before. And all because I had a bit of party!'

'They only went away for one night,' Jake reminded her. 'And the way I heard it—and not from Suzanne—you trashed the place.'

Abby grinned. 'Well, it did get a bit out of hand. But there was no need for our nosy neighbours to call out the cops.' And, straight on the heels of that, 'What are we doing tomorrow, Jake?'

Jake looked from Abby to Taryn. 'Unfortunately I have to go to Italy tomorrow.'

'Can I come?' Abby asked promptly.

'I have to work.'

'But it's Saturday!'

'I know,' he replied, but smiled as he added, 'I feel very hard done by—but a man must do what a man must do.'

'I think that's very unfair,' Abby opined sulkily.

'So do I,' he agreed. 'But I'll be home some time in the evening, and we'll have a lovely time on Sunday.'

Looking forward to Sunday, Abby went up to bed. Taryn went too, though was not totally surprised when a short while later her bedroom door opened and Jake came in. His glance swept over her, still dressed in smart trousers and top.

'I didn't ask you about Kate,' Taryn said, trying to appear as if she felt his visit was an everyday kind of happening. 'Is she all right?'

'I've never known her so well. Flourishing, in fact,' he replied, and enquired evenly, 'Not in bed yet?'

'I thought I'd wait until after your visit,' she replied, in much the same tone.

'It worries you—my coming into your room?'

You could say that again—though perhaps 'worry' wasn't quite the word she would have used. 'Good grief, no!' she denied, wanting dreadfully to ask if he was missing her at the office, but knowing that the idea he might say yes was laughable. 'I—er—expect the office is managing quite well without me?' was as far as she dared venture—and she was amazed to see Jake's easy look change to one of extreme annoyance.

'You're not thinking of taking Mellor up on his offer?' he grated forthrightly.

'What—?' she began, startled.

'He wants you to go back and work for him!' Jake rapped.

And all at once Taryn was feeling annoyed too. 'Well, of course he does!' she snapped. 'I was good.'

Belligerently she stared at him. Icily he stared back. 'Are you going to go back to him?' he demanded—and suddenly her heart was pounding.

'Are you saying you want to get rid of me?' she asked, hoping to hide her fear, but inwardly panicking.

'What the hell sort of question is that?'

She would not back down. 'You came in here looking for a fight!' she accused. 'I can only—'

'If I wanted to get rid of you I'd tell you outright, not wait for you to be upset and do the job for me,' he gritted, and Taryn began to feel better.

'So you would,' she murmured, having learned that much about him in the time she had been working for him. He could be more direct and to the point than anyone else she knew when he had to be. 'So what have I done to upset you?' she asked, her belligerency a thing of the past.

And all at once Jake appeared to relax. He even gave a shame-faced kind of grin as he came closer and acknowledged, 'It's not you, it's—' He broke off, took another couple of steps nearer, and said, 'I don't take kindly to having a valued member of my staff poached.'

Valued! Her heart lifted. 'Valued?' she murmured. 'You didn't say.'

He looked down at her. He was a foot or so away from her. 'I didn't think I had to.'

Perhaps he didn't at that. Unexpectedly her heart swelled with pride, and perhaps it was the intimacy of their surroundings, perhaps it was the fact that Jake had kissed her several times— Taryn did not stop to analyse what it was—but all of a sudden she gave in to an urge to do something she would never have done in an office environment. She took a step closer and, as he had done when he had come in that evening—only this time Abby wasn't present—Taryn stretched up and kissed him. Not on his cheek, nor in a lover's fashion, but on his lips.

'I'm sorry I misunderstood...' She was confused suddenly, and wasn't at all sure in her confusion what she was apologising for. She took a step back. 'I sh-shouldn't have done that,' she said in a rush. And loved it, loved him, when he smiled.

'It's the nicest apology I've had in a long while,' he replied softly.

Oh, grief—he looked as if he was about to return the compliment and kiss her. 'Goodnight, then,' she said abruptly, before he could take that step closer.

Jake halted. Then, taking hold of one of her hands, he brought it to his lips. 'You're a bit special, Taryn Webster,' he said, in a tone that made her bones melt. 'Do you know that?'

Desperately did she want to take that step forward again. And it took all the will she had to take another step back. 'I expect you'll have to be up early in the morning to catch your plane,' she said, from what brain she could find.

'And on that hint—I'll say goodnight,' Jake replied, but he was smiling.

Taryn was smiling too—long after he had gone. She was a valued member of his staff! She was still smiling as she got ready for bed. She had been an idiot not to realise that, she mused as she got into bed and lay down. It wasn't every member of staff that Jake brought into his home, was it?

But, and best of all, 'You're a bit special,' Jake had said. Oh, if only that was true and she *was* special—to him!

# CHAPTER SEVEN

JAKE left early the next morning. Taryn heard the door quietly close after him and quite desperately wanted to go with him to Italy—or anywhere. But he had not asked her to go with him, so he obviously had no need of a PA on this trip.

'Shopping?' she asked Abby, when later that morning Abby surfaced.

'I'm shopped out!' Abby declared, with a rare but genuine grin. But, setting her mind to what she wanted to do that lovely summer's day, 'Does your father live far from here?' she asked.

'Not too far,' Taryn replied cautiously—you never knew with Abby.

'Could we go and see him?'

'You want to visit my father?' Taryn asked, puzzled.

'He's a scientist,' Abby replied, and, looking a little embarrassed, 'I'm—um—sort of interested in anything like that. Would he mind, do you think, if we went and had a look at his latest project?'

Hoping that there wouldn't be any complications if her parent recalled that she worked for a Jake Nash—though she thought it more probable that her father, with his head in some other orbit, might not remember the name of where his daughter worked, 'I'm sure he'll be pleased to show you around,' Taryn answered.

As was proved when, a couple of hours later, she left Abby

doing the rounds of her father's workshops with him and went to say a courtesy hello to her stepmother. From what she had observed from the interest Abby was showing, and the intelligent questions she was asking, it was clear to Taryn that Jake's step-niece had a first class brain that would be utterly wasted should she opt to not go on to further education and a career.

As it happened, her stepmother was out at some charity all day bridge event. 'Would you mind if I made up a tray and some coffee, Mrs Ferris?' she asked their formidable housekeeper.

'Nice to be asked,' Mrs Ferris answered sniffily—but actually smiled.

Taryn made the housekeeper coffee as well, and was just about to carry the tray out when there was a ring at the doorbell. 'I'll get it,' she volunteered, and on opening the door was delighted to see her cousin standing there.

'Matt!' she beamed.

'Taryn!' he responded. 'I was hoping to catch you in. Doing anything tonight?'

Apparently Matt had dinner in mind. But by then Taryn was feeling a bit of a pull of loyalty to Abby, and she did not want to explain that she was keeping her boss's step-niece company because said step-niece had a crush on her step-uncle.

'Can't do, Matt. I'm sorry.'

'Had a better offer?'

'Actually, I'm—er—staying with Jake and his step-niece— er—at the moment,' she began.

'The second Mrs Webster getting too much?' he enquired, taking what she had just revealed in his stride.

'Jake's step-niece is here with me now. In the workshops,' she explained.

'But not Jake?'

'He's in Italy today.'

'He'd be the Jake of, "This is my boss, Jake Nash"?' Matt

asked, having been introduced to him on the night he had taken Taryn to his company's annual dinner-dance.

'That's—um...' Afraid of revealing too much, she couldn't finish.

But as Matt waited, and just looked at her, it seemed she already had. 'Oh, Taryn, love!' he said gently. 'The real thing this time?'

She wanted to deny it, but he knew her so well, and they had shared much in the past. 'It's all one-sided on my part, I'm afraid,' she confided.

'Taryn,' he mourned, knowing all about the pain of unrequited love. 'Tell me about it!'

'I've some coffee made. Have you got time for one?'

'More than that. Since you can't do dinner, how about I take you to lunch?'

Abby was enthralled by everything Horace Webster was showing her when Taryn and Matt, with the tray of coffee, caught up with them. Taryn made the introductions and Abby appeared delighted that Matt was taking them to lunch. Horace Webster declined Matt's invitation to go with them, but did leave his work for half an hour to be sociable.

Matt was good company. And while Taryn did not mention his wife Alison in front of Abby, Matt refrained from mentioning Jake—except to confirm, when asked by Abby, that the two had met.

It was a lovely meal time, and Taryn noticed that Abby seemed quite taken with Matt. Perhaps she was getting over her attachment to Jake?

It was in the early evening, however, when Taryn was starting to feel all churned up inside at the thought that Jake could walk in at any moment, that Abby gave her something else to concentrate her thoughts on.

Abby had been upstairs for quite some while, but when she joined her in the drawing room Taryn was startled to see how ashen-faced she was.

'I've just parted with my lunch,' she confessed wanly.

Taryn made her comfortable on the sofa, fetched her a drink of water, which was all she wanted, and set about gently questioning her.

Taryn's first thought was that something Abby had eaten at lunchtime had upset her. Then she recalled that she and Abby had ordered the same meal. Further questioning, though, revealed that Abby had woken up feeling a bit 'iffy', but had followed Suzanne's maxim to work off any aches and pains and 'you'll feel better by lunchtime'.

'I thought I did—feel better,' Abby explained. 'Only I don't now. In fact,' she went on, forcing a smile, 'I feel quite rubbishy. Oh, damn!' she suddenly exclaimed. 'I feel quite weepy with it. Don't let me cry when Jake gets home, will you?'

'He won't mind,' Taryn soothed.

'He might not, but I would!' Abby cried, managing another weak smile. 'I go all bung-eyed and blotchy when I cry—nothing film starry about me at all.'

'Would you like to go to bed?' Taryn offered. 'If you feel like something to eat later I can—'

'Don't!' Abby interjected hurriedly. 'Please, please don't mention food.'

Abby was starting to feel better when an hour later Jake arrived home. And, although she was still pale, she was not as ashen as she had been.

'Hello, you two,' he greeted them when, his eyes going straight to Taryn, he walked into the room. He was two strides in when he observed Abby's pallor. 'What happened to you?' he enquired.

'I've been Uncle Dick,' she adopted rhyming slang to tell him. 'But I feel better now.'

'What brought that on?'

'Nothing. Oh, please don't make a fuss. I'm all right now, really.'

Taryn got to her feet. 'Coffee?' she asked him, loving him, knowing how hard he worked and wanting to do any small thing she could to aid his day.

'Please,' he accepted, and a few minutes later joined her in the kitchen.

'Are you hungry?' she asked, looking up at him when he came close.

'Did you know you have the most fantastic blue, almost violet-coloured eyes?' he asked, apropos of nothing—and her heart thundered.

She sought for something clever with which to come back, but could come up with nothing other than, 'Would that be one slice of toast or two?'

His lips twitched, and he made her insides go all any-old-how when, every bit as if he could not resist it, he bent down and lightly kissed her on the lips. Hastily she pulled back—quite the opposite to what she instinctively wanted to do.

'Sorry,' he apologised, stepping away. 'I've sort of got into the habit of expecting Abby to appear out of nowhere,' he excused. And, while Taryn was berating herself for thinking anything so ridiculous such as that her lips might have been too tempting for him, he followed on, 'She's looking a bit peaky. Is she going to be all right?'

'I'll keep my eye on her, but I think she'll be fine. Though don't mention food in front of her.'

He nodded. Then asked, 'What are you having?'

'We had a big lunch,' she revealed, and went on to tell him of their day and of how her cousin had taken them to lunch.

'Did your father mind showing Abby around?'

'He was pleased to. He was quite tickled, I think, to have someone so young taking such a keen interest.' Taryn smiled as she stated, 'Actually, Abby is so bright it would be a great shame if she didn't train for something.'

'You might tell her that. Her father's been trying to get that through to her for a while now. According to Stuart she'd take it better from anyone but him.'

Taryn hadn't realised that Abby was so lacking in confidence, and realised too that she had grown to quite like the seventeen-year-old. 'I will if I get the chance,' she replied, and suddenly became aware that she had not taken her eyes off Jake in quite some while. It was a joy just to be standing there with him.

She looked quickly away, just as he suggested, 'Shall we eat our beans on toast in here?'

'That's all you want? Beans on toast?'

His eyes swept over her, and for one totally ridiculous moment she thought he was about to say that he wanted her. 'I too had a massive meal at lunchtime,' was all he replied.

Taryn went to bed that night knowing that she was going to have to curb her imagination. First of all she had thought he had kissed her because he could not help but do so—where on earth was her brain? Then she had thought, had *actually* thought, he had been about to say that he wanted *her!* Oh, for crying out loud, this love business was making an absolute nonsense of her otherwise sane head.

Because Abby was not a particularly early riser, and because it was after all Sunday morning, Taryn tapped lightly on her door at nine, when she had not surfaced—Jake was already 'tidying up a few things' in his study.

'How are you feeling today?' she asked as she went in. Abby was lying on her side, not looking very much better than she had last night.

She struggled to sit up. 'Trying to remember I'm Suzanne's step-daughter.'

'You don't have to try to work it off today,' Taryn said gently. 'Why not lie there for a bit? I can bring you breakfast up if—'

'Nuh-uh!' Abby cut in.

'Not hungry?'

Abby nodded. 'I don't want to be a nuisance, or you and Jake won't have me to stay again.'

'Oh, Abby,' Taryn murmured. 'You can't help being poorly.'

Then, recalling that Abby got tearful with sympathy, 'I'll get you something to drink.' And added, when it looked as if Abby might protest, 'It won't be the smallest trouble.'

Jake had left his study when Taryn went downstairs. He followed her into the kitchen. 'I thought we'd take a drive into the country, have lunch somewhere green and hilly and—' He broke off at Taryn's doubtful look. 'Not a good idea?'

'Abby's still a bit under the weather.'

'Anything I should worry about?'

'I don't think so. She's not interested in food, but would probably benefit from a quiet day,' Taryn suggested. And volunteered, 'I can cook you a roast, if you like. Though you'd have to go out with a shopping list.' That notion amused her.

'What's so funny?' he wanted to know.

Taryn controlled herself. 'While I think it would be a good idea to get you away from an office environment for a while, the idea of the chairman of the Nash Corporation pushing a trolley around a supermarket doesn't seem to fit you somehow.'

'You're saying I couldn't do it?'

She laughed, knowing he had taken the bait, the challenge. 'Sucker!' she murmured—and found herself suddenly grabbed hold of and caught up in the most delicious bear-hug.

'Ooh!' she squealed—and loved him to bits.

'This is how you get my drink?' enquired a voice from the doorway.

Jake glanced over, but still had his arms around Taryn. He transferred his gaze back to her dark blue eyes. 'I'll deal with you later,' he said, and kissed the tip of her nose.

It might all have been done on account of Abby being there, but Taryn had never known herself so flustered. It took her all of fifteen minutes to get herself back together—it had all seemed so spontaneous somehow.

Abby spent most of the day on a sofa, swearing she was feeling better and better each time she caught Taryn checking on her. To Taryn's mind she did not look any better and, having—incredible as it seemed to her—sent her boss out with a small shopping list, she prepared a meal, knowing that if Abby wasn't showing any signs of improving by morning she would be taking her to see a doctor.

Jake had returned from his shopping expedition with magazines and papers for his two guests. It did not surprise Taryn, though, that, having stayed in the drawing room with them to read his own papers, he should then go and spend time in his study.

He must be hating like crazy having his privacy invaded like this, she mused. He must be counting the hours until next Tuesday, when his sister and her husband returned and he could have his home back to himself.

Taryn vowed then that she would keep out of his way as much as possible in the time remaining of his sister's holiday. But she could only love him more that he had put his sister's request to have Abby stay before his own preference not to be so invaded.

They were all in the drawing room that evening, but it was still in Taryn's mind to keep out of his way. Though since his study appeared to have more appeal that hadn't been difficult. 'I think I'll have an early night,' she decided, getting to her feet.

'I'll come up too, I think,' Abby said, and, having eaten barely anything that day, left the sofa. 'Night, Jake,' she said, so cheerfully that Taryn just knew she was feeling really poorly.

'I'll be up in a minute or two,' Taryn told her, when Abby waited for her.

'Oh—you two lovebirds.' Abby grinned, but took the hint and went from the room.

'So,' Jake began, coming over to where Taryn stood, Abby now out of earshot, 'given that I've thanked you for the best meal I've eaten all week, and given that I somehow have the sad feeling that you don't find me totally irresistible…'

'In your dreams,' she lied.

'What did you want to see me about?'

'Abby,' Taryn replied without preamble. 'If she's not better tomorrow, I think I should take her to see a doctor.'

'You believe she's that unwell?' Jake was instantly alert.

'I'd feel happier if she was checked over. It may be just a bug that's doing the rounds, but…'

'Do you want me to come with you?'

Taryn smiled what she hoped was a reassuring smile. 'I think we can manage that on our own. But is it all right if I ring you at the office if—'

'Of course it is,' he cut in straight away. 'Ring me anyway, to let me know how you get on.' But all at once he had stilled, and was looking into her upturned face. 'You truly are lovely—in mind as well as body,' he said softly.

Oh, heavens, she was going to melt. 'May my halo never slip!' she managed to mock, and while she still had the strength she got out of there.

Taryn found it extremely difficult to get to sleep that night—Jake had previously called her beautiful; Jake thought her lovely in mind and body! Having gone to bed early, it seemed ages before thoughts of Jake—her wonderful, wonderful Jake, but not hers at all—were replaced by sleep. And barely had she fallen asleep, it seemed, than Abby was in her room, saying she felt a touch not so good.

Taryn groggily reached for the light switch and was instantly out of bed. Abby, she could see for herself, looked quite ghastly. 'Have you any pain?' she asked, getting Abby to sit down in a padded bedroom chair.

'A bit of a nasty tummy ache.'

'Where, exactly?' Taryn asked, thinking appendicitis but unable to remember if that was the right side or left.

'All over, really,' Abby replied.

'Have you been sick again?'

'A bit,' Abby answered.

She had barely eaten anything, so there would not have been much to bring back, Taryn considered. But trying not to be alarmist, there were alarm bells going off in her head that prompted the snippet—and she had no idea how she knew it— that if appendicitis wasn't seen to, it could lead to peritonitis!

'Hang on here. I won't be a minute,' she said, and, shrugging into her cotton wrap, she went quickly along the landing to Jake's room.

She might have knocked on his door—she wasn't thinking too clearly of anything but that Abby was in a spot of trouble—but to her surprise Jake's light was on and, bare-chested, he was sitting up in bed reading. A glance to his bedside clock showed it had just gone midnight. Good heavens—she had thought it much, much later.

'Taryn!' he exclaimed, his book going down, the covers going back.

She caught a glimpse of a long length of leg and had a panicky idea that he was naked. Hurriedly she turned about. Two hands descended on her shoulders and he turned her to face him.

'Abby,' she said in a rush, taking a gasp of breath. Somehow he had found time to throw on a robe. 'She's in my room, not at all well. She's playing it down, but I think she's in quite some pain.'

He stayed calm. 'Any idea what might be wrong?'

'It could be her appendix. Can we call out a doctor? I'd rather not wait until morning.'

'If you're thinking appendix, I'm thinking hospital.' He smiled reassuringly into Taryn's worried eyes. 'Give me two minutes. I'll get dressed and take her in.'

Taryn could not help but feel relieved that Jake was taking charge. 'I'll get dressed and come with you,' she replied.

He shook his head. 'There's no need for us all to lose sleep. If you could just get her ready?'

No way. No way were they going without her!

It seemed impossible that so much could happen in such a short space of time, but by half past one she and Jake were back home.

It did not seem right to have left Abby in hospital but Taryn knew that she was in the best place.

Having been looked at, questioned, poked and prodded, the diagnosis had been a severe gastro upset, and not appendicitis. But just in case, they were keeping Abby in hospital under observation.

'Shall I make a drink?' Taryn asked.

'I'll do it.'

She went to the kitchen with him. 'I'm sorry if you thought I was being alarmist.' She felt she should apologise.

'Hey!' Jake pulled her up. 'I saw Abby too, remember? We just couldn't leave her in pain and feeling so ill and do nothing. As it was I was wondering if I should make a phone call to Stuart.'

'You decided to wait until we'd got a diagnosis?'

'He worries about her enough as it is. I didn't want to add to that load unless I had to.'

'He'd have come home?'

'Next plane.'

Taryn smiled at him, but with Abby safely tucked up in hospital it suddenly hit her with a most unhappy force that there was no earthly reason for her to remain.

'I'd—um—better get my belongings together,' she said out of nowhere, by far preferring to go of her own accord rather than have Jake hint she was now superfluous to requirements.

'Belongings?' he echoed, for all the world as if he had no idea of what she was talking about. But as he cottoned on his expression became stern, and he abandoned his coffee-making to bluntly demand, 'What for?'

Why was he making her feel that she was in the wrong? 'Well—there's no need for me to be here now that—'

'There's every need,' he cut in sharply.

'Why?' She did not care very much for his tone—though hers was not much sweeter.

'Why—because—the hospital may ring. They may want me to go and pick Abby up!' he said toughly.

'In the middle of the night?'

'I don't want you to go!' he rapped angrily.

Oh, if only that had sounded as though for himself he did not want her to go, and not because he might have some semi-invalid on his inexperienced hands.

'Huh!' she retorted, which meant nothing but conveyed, she hoped, that she did not care to be spoken to that way. 'Forget the coffee!' she snapped, and, feeling weepy suddenly, and hating him and her love for him that it could bring her to this, she stormed out from the kitchen.

In her room, she fumed against him. So, okay, they were both tired, and had been through a fraught hour and a half—but, honestly, who did he think he was with his 'I don't want you to go'? As if, having said that, his word was law and she had better obey.

For two pins she would go right now. Against that—she loved the bossy swine. But no matter; she was leaving in the morning. She was positive about that. For all she knew Abby could be in hospital for a couple of days or more. What was she supposed to do if that happened? Sit around here twiddling her thumbs?

Taryn had changed into her night things, but was still feeling a trifle anti one Jake Nash when there was a knock on her door.

Good of him to knock, she sniffed, reaching for her wrap. Although with no Abby there to chance observing anything that might give a clue that she and Jake were not as close as they were making out to be, Taryn thought that to knock instead of just walking in was more in keeping.

As she went to answer his knock, she was not prepared to concede him any good points—talking to her the way he had!

'If you think I'm taking down shorthand at this time of night...' she began hostilely, trying to stifle the happy realisation that she might well be doing that in about ten hours' time—in his office.

Jake was still dressed, she noticed, and any further hostile words faded when, not a bit put off by her hostility, he smiled.

She was on the way to melting before he volunteered, 'I'm a brute.'

Backbone, backbone—remember your backbone. 'True,' she replied coolly. 'Do you want to go on to the next question?'

His mouth quirked upwards again. 'The next question is—are you going to forgive me?'

She looked at him, looked up into his twinkling grey eyes, eyes that somehow did not seem too sorry, and her heart seemed to tip over. She had to end this here and now—he was making a nonsense of her. 'You're forgiven,' she replied tartly, and went to close the door on him.

His hand against it stopped her. 'That didn't sound very forgiving,' he commented.

As if he wouldn't sleep for what was left of the rest of the night if she didn't say it nicely! She was smiling inwardly; she knew that she was. 'You're forgiven,' she repeated, though much more softly this time.

Jake took a step away. But then, every bit as if he did not want to go yet—and how fanciful was that?—he stepped nearer again. 'Forgive me properly,' he said.

She stared at him, uncomprehending for a moment or two. Then she saw his glance go down to her mouth, and suddenly, as her heart set up an almighty clamouring, she thought she knew what he meant.

'Oh, no,' she said huskily, backing away.

She was in her room, he had followed, his eyes now on her eyes, never leaving. 'Are you sure about that?' he enquired, his voice all bone-melting and will-sapping.

'You do realise what time it is?' She had no idea herself just then, but was struggling to find strength.

'You've kissed me before—I wasn't even expecting it then,' he reminded her.

'There were—um—extenuating circumstances then,' she reminded him, for the life of her having not the slightest memory just then of what those circumstances had been, other than that possibly Abby might have been around at the time. 'Oh!' Taryn exclaimed impatiently, snappily, and did not know who she was impatient with—Jake or herself.

Whatever, thinking to give him a peck and get it over with, she reached up and kissed his cheek, lost her balance—and just had to hang on to him for a moment.

At least, a moment was all it was supposed to have been. But she loved him. And he was warm, and somehow those arms that had come out to hold her steady were somehow around her, and Jake was looking down into her darkened dark blue eyes.

'I won't hurt you,' he said softly.

'I—trust you,' she replied, feeling more than a touch spellbound.

And he smiled, and he kissed her. 'That wasn't so bad, was it?' he asked, pulling back from his gentle kiss.

'Actually,' she murmured, and swallowed hard, 'it was—er— quite nice.'

'You're a bit of a darling,' he teased.

So kiss me again. 'Would I argue?' she asked lightly, glad he was holding her. She had an idea she would crumple in a heap at his feet if he wasn't. 'Er—goodnight, then,' said the treacherous person inside her who would deprive her of these moments in Jake's arms.

'Goodnight, darling,' he bade her, oh so tenderly, and gathered her to him for one last kiss.

Only it was not a last kiss. Because the moment his lips touched hers, so Taryn lost the small amount of control he had left her with. Her arms went around him and he—he did not object at all. His kiss deepened, and Taryn did not know anything—other than that his arms fitted as though they had been made for her, and she never wanted him to let her go.

She held on to him, loving every moment when his arms tightened about her and he brought her closer and closer to him. She could feel his all male body through the thinness of her clothing, and as he pressed to her, so she pressed into him.

'You know that I want you?' he asked, raising his head from a kiss that had left her breathless.

'Y-yes,' she answered shakily.

His kissed her again, sending her into raptures as he trailed kisses down the side of her throat. 'And—how do you feel about that?' he asked.

Taryn kissed him. She was in a world she had never been in before. But what could she tell him? She loved him, was in love with him, and to make love with him just seemed—so right.

'I—um—think you know,' she answered shyly.

And knew that he did when he cried her name. 'Taryn!' And the next time he kissed her, she just knew that there was no going back. Which was wonderful—she did not want to go back.

As he kissed her, so she returned his kisses. Somehow her wrap had disappeared, his shirt too, and Jake was holding her close to him, his gently caressing hands moving over her back, burning through the thin cotton of her camisole top.

Then, to make her momentarily stiffen, she felt those same hands on her bare skin, beneath her camisole. 'Don't worry, sweetheart,' Jake soothed tenderly, his hands at her back momentarily still.

'I'm not worried,' she answered, trying not to be brazen, but fearing he might stop. 'Just a bit shy, I think.'

'Little love,' he murmured, and as his mouth closed over hers once more, so his hands, his sensitive fingers, tenderly, slowly, breath-holdingly sweetly, caressed their gentle way up to her breasts.

'Jake, oh, Jake,' she whispered.

'It's all right,' he gentled her.

And it was all right. More than all right. Somehow he had dispensed with his trousers, and as she felt his bare thighs against her, felt his wanting body against her, so a fire started to rage out of control within her. And so Taryn began to part with each and all of her inhibitions. Even when Jake removed her camisole, the better to see, to kiss and to mould her beautiful breasts, not a murmur did she make, save to shyly confess, 'I want you, Jake.'

Exultantly, he caught her to him. Kissed her eyes, her mouth, her throat, her breasts, taking in turn each hardened pink tip into his mouth.

And as he enjoyed her nakedness so Taryn, released of her inhibitions, absolutely adored the freedom he allowed as she stroked his broad manly chest, and in turn kissed and tasted his nipples.

She was in some enchanted land when Jake led her over to the bed. 'Let me remember again,' he breathed, and it was only when he slid his hands inside her pyjama shorts and started to remove then that she understood.

Jake had seen her naked once before. That time she had made use of his private shower. 'I…!' She all of a sudden found that she did have a few inhibitions left after all. 'Jake. N-no.' She stopped him, and could do nothing about the hint of alarm in her voice.

That hint was sufficient to give him pause, however. With his hands, his touch, burning on her naked hips, he halted. 'Taryn?' He said her name, a question there in his voice. He pulled back to look into her face, saw the scarlet colour searing her skin—and suddenly, as though scalded, he was snatching his hands from her, putting some space between them. Catching up her cotton wrap, he hastily draped it round her. 'My God, what am I thinking of?' he exclaimed hoarsely.

'It's all right!' Taryn told him urgently. She wanted him, desperately wanted him, and knew that he wanted her—but had the most frightening feeling that he had suddenly gone off the idea of making love to her. 'What's wrong?' she asked. And hurried to assure him, 'I didn't mean "No" no, just…'

'I'm taking advantage of this situation,' he said, getting into his trousers and zipping them up.

Take it, she wanted to beg. Take advantage. But she knew then, as he took as step to the door, that it was over. And could only thank heaven for pride. 'You're afraid I won't respect you in the morning?' she accused lightly, but was mystified to know how, when her skin was still burning from their intimacy. From somewhere she even found a bit of a laugh.

Jake stared at her, looked at her as though he might well take her back in his arms. But he had better control than her—Taryn would have returned to the haven of his arms like a shot, had he offered.

But he did not offer, but said jerkily, 'I'm going.' And was gone.

# CHAPTER EIGHT

SHE had slept little. It was still early, but Taryn saw no point in staying in bed. She showered and got dressed and began collecting her belongings together. She was well and truly back down to earth.

Never, ever would she forget those sensational kisses she had shared with Jake. But in the cold light of day she was forced to face the unpalatable truth. And that truth, painful though it was to face, was that while she had been absolutely mindless to anything but him, and had been his for the taking, he had not been so similarly affected. How could he have been, to walk away from her the way he had?

Taryn started to panic—had he seen that she loved him? Oh, she just couldn't bear it if he had. She heard sounds that told her he was moving around, and knew that soon she was going to have to face him. She quite desperately wanted to just slip out from his home without seeing him. Then she held her breath when she thought she heard him on the landing, thought she heard him pause outside her door. She was mistaken and, straining her ears, the next sounds she heard were his fading footsteps as he went on down the stairs.

She realised right then that she was going to have to curb her imagination. It was no good wishing or imagining what was or what might have been. She must think only in facts. Fact—she had been willing. Fact—he had said no thank you. He might have called her darling—in the heat of the moment might even have called her sweetheart, little love. But was that a declaration of love? Fact—no, it jolly well wasn't. And she would be an idiot to imagine he might love her a tiny bit.

My heavens, the fates must be laughing! What was she thinking of anyway, to imagine that Jake might have some small caring for her? He had not given so much as a tiny hint that he thought anything of her other than that she was reasonable at her job and convenient when he needed assistance when he found it difficult to say no to his sister.

Taryn became aware that she was starting to bridle, starting to feel more than a little miffed where he was concerned. Good—she needed all the help she could get. Feeling quite belligerent all of a sudden, that feeling gave her strength to leave her room and go in search of him.

He was in the kitchen fixing himself some coffee when she went in. He had his back to her. Taryn seized the moment while she still could—he was so... Stop it! He wasn't dear at all. 'I'm leaving this morning,' she addressed his back crisply.

He swung about, his eyes going over her. If he noticed the mauvish circles under her eyes from lack of sleep he refrained from commenting, but asked evenly enough, 'What brought this on?'

Honestly. As if he didn't know. Taryn could feel her emotions going out of control and fought to stay on top of them. 'I—just think it's best I leave,' she replied, as calmly as she could.

His look was gentle, tender almost. 'Because of last night?' he enquired. 'Because—?'

But that was just too much. How dared he reject her and then have the infernal nerve to unemotionally refer to it? 'I—' she cut in, hot about the ears and dying a thousand deaths. She did not want a debate about it! She was in love with him, and...

'You regret—' he started to cut in too.

'Yes, I do. I very much regret it,' she informed him coldly, hoping her tone would put an end to the discussion. Fat chance! She should have known from working with him that when he wanted to know something he went right to the root.

His eyes narrowed. He did not seem to be enjoying this, and certainly not her cold tone, any more than she was. 'It worries you to have discovered that you're a perfectly healthy woman with a woman's perfectly healthy appetite for—'

'I don't want to go to bed with you!' she rushed in bluntly. Honestly, this was just more than too much. Though if he came back with something equally blunt—such as, *My, how you've changed*—she was going to hit him.

He did not come back with anything of the sort, but his tone had lost its softer edge when shortly he questioned, 'You feel—ashamed—that last night you were so willing?' And, his look alert, sharp and totally unsmiling, 'You feel—cheapened in some way?' he demanded.

'I don't want...' she sped in. Oh, heavens above—how had they ever got started on this? 'What I *do* want—' she attempted to put the conversation back where she wanted it '—is a career. I want to hone my skills and be the best PA I can be. And... And...' She was running out of steam. 'And...' she tried again, still floundering.

'And?' Jake prompted, his expression stern all at once, not helping her out at all.

'And...' she took up, and it all came out in a rush then. 'And I don't think it's appropriate for me to—' She came to an abrupt stop.

But Jake was not waiting. 'You don't think it appropriate to make love with your boss?' he cut in.

She did not think her cheeks would ever cool down. But, spurred on by the unwanted truth that said boss had declined the offer, all she had left was a hope to screen that she loved him, and a hope to make him see that from the very fact they had to work together their relationship had to be purely business.

'You must see that for yourself,' she retorted. 'Matters got out of hand last night. And, no, the last thing I want is to go to bed with you,' she replied loftily—that or sink. But she did not care for the hostile way he was suddenly looking at her—even though she realised she had probably brought that on herself with her cold and uppity way of speaking. 'There may be times when I have to go away with you,' she forced herself to go on. 'Times when... Well, it isn't what I want, and I have more regard for myself than to—'

'Aside from the fact that it was me who walked away?' he curtly cut in to trounce her, his tone toughening. 'You, this morning, consider my lovemaking offensive?' he questioned harshly. Oh, my love, No! No. No. *No!* But he wasn't waiting for an answer, but suggested categorically, his tone cutting, 'It's a pity you didn't realise that last night when you were giving me the green welcome-to-my-bed light all the way.'

She nearly died on the spot. But that last remark had well and truly put paid to any weakening that had been trying to surface in her. Taryn did not thank him for the reminder—no reminder necessary—that *he* had been the one to do the walking. But—and thank you very much, Mr Nash—what he had done was give her the extra strength she needed to rubbish any ridiculous notion he might have gleaned of her true feeling for him.

'It's never going to happen anyway,' she told him frostily, for all the world as if the choice was hers. But her frosty remark had not gone down well, she could tell. Ice chips were forming in his eyes and he was looking most decidedly anti one Taryn Webster. Oh, my word, she'd made him angry—most definitely time to change the subject! 'You'll um—be telephoning the hospital later, I expect?'

Jake favoured her with a grim look. 'I already did,' he gritted shortly.

'What...?' Taryn began, when it did not look as if he was going to share the latest news on Abby.

'It appears to definitely not be appendicitis,' he replied icily. 'Abby will be home today.'

'Oh!' Taryn's determination to leave started to fracture, albeit that it was not very affably that she asked, 'You want me to wait here for her?'

'Don't bother!' Jake rapped, before she could draw another breath. And, his look like flint, 'I don't need you as much as I thought I did,' he informed her stingingly.

Taryn's mouth fell open in shock. And as she blanched Jake seemed to take a step towards her. But, as if recalling how he had taken a step towards her last night—and look what had happened—the next step he took was to walk straight past her.

She heard his study door close with a determined thud and guessed that he was checking his briefcase before departing to a business which he could not have said more clearly she had no part in.

Smarting, close to tears, Taryn hastened from the kitchen and up to her room.

She stayed there until she heard him leave the house. He had not come back up the stairs to see her. Why would he? Somehow or other her simple statement that she was leaving that morning had got out of hand. And all she had done in her efforts to hide from him the way he could make her heart sing was to end up making him angry.

Jake had his pride too. She recognised that. With him believing she felt she would be cheapened if she went to bed with him, it was, she supposed, pretty near guaranteed to ensure he would have to let her know who was who.

And he'd done that, hadn't he? 'I don't need you as much as I thought I did' might have been intended to convey he could well cope with his step-niece unaided, but Taryn knew it conveyed more than that. As in, *Don't ring me, I'll ring you.* As in, *Only don't hold your breath.* As in, *There are plenty more PAs to pick and choose from.*

Taryn was still shaken to know she was out of a job. It hurt. The thought of never seeing Jake again was too painful to bear. She contemplated, but only briefly, going into the office to see what happened. Would he really throw her out on her ear? Or would he, perhaps having cooled down, accept he had been a little bit hasty?

Forget it. She knew full well—love him though she did, hurt at the thought of never seeing him again though she might—that it just was not in her to be dismissed—because that in effect was what had happened—and then go crawling to Jake to ask for her job back. He could stuff his job, she thought on a wave of mutiny— but she was crying on the inside.

With her packing completed, spurred on by the thought that Mrs Vincent would be arriving round about nine, Taryn left the key Jake had given her on his study table and got out of there.

She guessed he would be in touch with Mrs Vincent to ask her to keep an eye on Abby while he was at work. He might even ask Mrs Vincent to extend her hours. Taryn had no idea what was a normal time for patients to be allowed out of hospital, but she was positive that Jake would break off from his day to go to the hospital to collect Abby. And in any event his sister and Abby's father would be home tomorrow.

Taryn knew it was too late now to regret any of what she had done. Too late to regret that it all got so out of hand. The reason for that, she supposed, was that basically her emotions were still in something of an uproar—and had been ever since Jake had come to her room last night.

So much for her thinking that this morning would see her in his office, taking down his dictation. She paused briefly to wonder how Kate would manage. But Kate seemed to be through that very bad patch, and, whatever happened, it would not take Jake long to get someone to assist Kate if he thought it necessary. Certainly there would be someone taking her place well before Kate went on maternity leave. Taryn was positive of that.

Realising that she had been driving along without any particular mind to where she was going, Taryn recognised suddenly that she was heading in the direction of her aunt's offices.

She pulled over to the side of the road. It did not seem fair that she made for her aunt Hilary every time she was upset. Her home was none too welcoming, but at least she wouldn't be called upon to skivvy when she got there.

Though a couple of hours later, with not a thing to do, Mrs Ferris having politely declined her offer of help, Taryn was staring out of her bedroom window, ready to welcome a spot of skivvying. It was not her way to sit idle, and she was fast forming the opinion that she would go potty if she did not soon find something to do. And this was only her first day of being unemployed!

She had too much time to think. Especially did she have too much time to think when all she seemed able to think about was Jake Nash, his lovemaking, the utter joy of being in his arms—and the discordant way her relationship with him had that morning ended.

And it was all her fault! He had been pleasant enough until she had rattled him. Had she been more in control of her emotions, and perhaps not so anxious to hide any sign that she had feelings for him, then it all might have ended very differently. But, no, she had… Oh, stop it, do—think about something else.

It was mid-afternoon when, in her attempts to pin her thoughts on something else, Taryn recalled she had told Brian Mellor she would give him a ring. She struggled with her conscience for a few minutes. After Jake no way did she want to go back and work for Brian. But, while aware now of what being in love felt like, and having recognised that she had never been in love with Brian, she was still fond of him.

Jake was back in her head again. In a hasty endeavour to oust him from her thoughts, Taryn grabbed up the phone and rang Mellor Engineering. Inside no time she had Brian's delighted voice in her ear.

'Where are you working now?' he asked, after warmly greeting her.

'Er—I'm not at the moment.'

'I could do with you here,' he said promptly. 'I've a new PA started today, but I can switch her to another department. Just say the word.'

No way did she want to do that to the poor girl, whoever she was. 'Um—I'm taking a break from being a PA at the moment, Brian,' Taryn explained. That the break was being forced on her was something she had no wish to confide.

'You're sure?' he pressed, and went on to say how the office was in a bit of a mess, his two previous PAs both having left in quick succession. 'If you're sure you don't want to come back on a permanent basis, how would you feel—as a favour to me— about coming in on a temporary basis? You know the work,' he urged. 'If you could come in just to clear the backlog, and show Lucy, my new PA, the ropes?'

With the words 'favour' and 'temporary' rolling around in her head, Jake was back in residence. 'Yes,' she said quickly, more trying to block out Jake's image than being interested in the temporary job on offer.

'You will?' He sounded overjoyed.

'I'll see you tomorrow,' she said, before she should change her mind.

'Great!' Brian enthused.

Taryn put down the phone, knowing that she was committed. Too late now to backtrack. But, on thinking about it, perhaps to be by the sound of it very busy clearing a backlog of work, was not such a bad thing? So why did she feel she was being disloyal to Jake in going to work for someone else? It was for sure he'd find the notion highly humorous.

Taryn awoke on Tuesday and felt an almost undeniable urge to ring Jake's home and enquire how Abby was. Abby had turned out to be far nicer than she had first appeared. But Taryn resisted the urge.

Jake would just love it, wouldn't he, that, having walked out on her assignment, she had the gall to enquire after Abby's health? Not that she would have phoned while he was there. Taryn sniffed proudly.

Within an hour of working for Brain, it was as if she had never been away. The work was easy. Only then did she appreciate how much she had learned when working for the Nash Corporation. How much... Stop it. That phase of her life was over. Bleak though that fact was, it was true.

Taryn concentrated all her energies on helping Lucy Reid, Brian's new PA. She was a competent woman of about twenty-eight, who had a quick brain. Taryn felt she would make out very well.

In fact they were doing so well that Taryn could see that she would not be needed for more than a couple of days. Something which, happening to be in Brian's office, she thought to mention.

'Finish the week out, anyway?' he requested, reluctant, it seemed, to let her go. 'You brighten up my otherwise dull life.'

'If that's what you'd like,' she agreed. He looked tired, as if he wasn't sleeping well. 'I was—um—sorry to hear about you and Angie.' She hadn't wanted to bring it up, but it seemed as if he wanted to talk about it. 'You always seemed so devoted.'

'That's what I thought,' he replied straight away, going on, when Taryn did not want to pry, 'That was until I discovered that Angie was having an affair...' Angie? Quiet Angie, having an affair! 'I was as shocked as you look,' Brian commented. 'I just never thought she would—much less suspected it. Apparently I spent too much time in the office. Anyhow, she promised not to see him again, and we tried to make a go of it—but it was never on.'

'I'm so sorry,' Taryn said genuinely.

'Me too,' he sighed. 'It seems Angie fell out of love with me and in love with lover-boy.'

'So she left?'

He shook his head, and, proving to be the kind and good person she had always thought him to be, 'I couldn't do that to her and the children. I left. Though I admit I felt a bit of a patsy when I heard that he had moved in.'

It was as if, having got started, Brian needed to talk out some of his pain. And, out of the affection and friendship she had for him, Taryn, without saying a word against Angie, let him carry on talking some of the hurt out of his system.

'I suppose I must have been at my very lowest that day I—um—kissed you,' he confessed. 'Everything had gone cold on me—I just wanted some human warmth. But I should never have done what I did. It was—'

'Water under the bridge, Brian,' she butted in. 'Gone and forgotten,' she said—and went home that night feeling not a little fed up with life in general. Brian was unhappy, she was unhappy—loving someone who did not love you was the pits.

To add to the gloom of unrequited love, her lovely cousin Matt rang her that night. 'I wasn't sure if you'd returned home,' he said cheerfully. 'I'm off abroad again for six months on Thursday. Fancy having dinner with me before I go?'

'Love to,' she answered, and made arrangements for the following evening. But she knew as she put down the phone that for Matt to be going away for six months must mean that he had accepted that, with Alison starting divorce proceedings, his marriage was well and truly over. On that depressing thought, she went to bed.

She did not want to put in an appearance at Mellor Engineering when she got up. But she had given her word to stay until this coming Friday, so made her way there and spent a busy day clearing more of the backlog and instructing Lucy when required.

Dinner with Matt that evening was a much more cheerful affair than she had anticipated. He was surprised that she had left the Nash Corporation, though. 'I thought you were hoping for bigger and better things?' he remarked.

'That'll teach me.'

'Your leaving's all tied up with your feelings for Jake Nash?' he guessed.

'He doesn't know.'

'I won't tell him,' Matt confided comically, and they both grinned.

'Alison?' Taryn asked. 'I take it you haven't heard from her directly?'

'I went round, but—' He broke off, looked desolate for a moment, but, as ever putting a brave face on it, 'It'll all come out in the wash,' he said with a smile, then urged, 'Come on, let's drown our sorrows and get tiddly.'

They tried, but were both near enough stone-cold sober when Matt hailed a taxi. Being in love—he with Alison, she with Jake—seemed to put a blight on everything.

Come Thursday, and Taryn made gigantic efforts to put Jake out of her head. It was not easy. Ever since she had left his home on Monday she was reminded of him everywhere. Any business suited man around the same height could trigger memories of him. She seemed to see him in any tall man with dark hair; her stomach would knot on the instant, then the man would turn around—and it was never Jake.

Having caught up on the backlog, and having seen for herself that Lucy Reid was well on the way to coping without her help, by three o'clock on Friday Taryn had formed the opinion that, with nothing left for her to do, her presence in Brian's offices was more of a hindrance than a help.

'I'm off,' she told him, on going in to see him.

'You're sure you don't want to come back? If not to this office, you'd be an asset to any...'

But Taryn was shaking her head. 'I'm not sure I want to be a PA.' And with that, and from the affection she had for him, she went over to him and kissed his cheek. 'I hope things get better for you soon,' she said quietly, and went to say goodbye to Lucy.

Taryn was walking to the lifts when she began to wonder what she would do now. Perhaps, she deliberated as she waited for the lift to answer her call, she would have a chat to Aunt Hilary and discuss the possibility of doing some temp work.

She halted that thought right there. Aunt Hilary had found her a job working for Osgood Compton—and look what had happened.

The lift seemed a long time in coming. But just as she was thinking she would take the stairs it arrived.

The doors opened and her heart fluttered as she caught the sketchiest glimpse of a dark haired, business suited man as several people got out and she got in. She ignored him and faced the front. The lift stopped at the next floor and someone else got out, which left just her and the tall man. But as the lift started to descend, so she felt his eyes boring into her. Certain she was imagining it, she glanced up—and very nearly went into heart failure. The man *was* Jake Nash!

Her jaw dropped in shock. He seemed pretty shaken too, she observed. In fact he seemed to have lost some of his colour as speechlessly he stared at her. Then suddenly she noticed that there was a pulse banging away in his temple.

She was still desperately searching for some kind of greeting— or not, since he did not seem inclined to acknowledge her—when she saw his colour start to return, and with it some kind of angry emotion.

And what she did say was a totally involuntary repeat of the very first words he had ever said to her, 'You seem—upset?' she murmured huskily.

His stare turned into a furious glare, and as the lift stopped at the ground floor, 'You've got a bloody nerve!' he grated harshly.

Taryn blinked in astonishment. 'What have I done?' she asked in bewilderment.

But he was angry. Oh, my heavens, he was angry. She couldn't miss seeing that! 'You can come with me and I'll tell you,' he snarled, and as the doors opened he caught a hold of her arm in a vice-like grip and ushered her out and towards the main doors.

They were at his parked car before Taryn was anywhere near recovered. 'What—?' she attempted to protest.

'Leave it!' he barked. 'Get in!' he rapped, opening the passenger door.

'Really!' she exclaimed, refusing to budge. Her heart might be dancing a jig to be this close to him when she had never expected to see him again. But...

He pulled the passenger door open wider. 'In!' he commanded, his tone, his look, all stating that he was not prepared to take any nonsense.

Her knees suddenly went boneless. Jake Nash all too plainly wanted to sort her out about something. She got into his car. For the moment she felt weak enough to let him try.

# CHAPTER NINE

THE car was in motion and Jake was driving in the thick of traffic before Taryn had got herself anywhere near together. 'What did I do?' she turned to ask his stony profile. He ignored her. She did not like it. 'Where are we going?' she persisted— another waste of breath. 'Look here…' she began to erupt, feeling more than a touch nervous but starting to get angry herself. He was looking nowhere but straight in front.

She might have persisted further, but then she started to recognise the route they were travelling. He couldn't possibly be taking her back to the Nash Corporation building—could he?

It seemed he could. Inside the next ten minutes he had parked in the bay reserved for him and was coming round to the passenger door. He opened the door, but Taryn, even if her heart was in overdrive, sat determinedly where she was and favoured him with a frosty look.

Jake looked grimly back, and took a long indrawn breath. 'I'm in no mood to play games,' he warned her icily. 'You have precisely thirty seconds to step out of this car.'

Mulishly she stayed put. But that was when her treacherous other self, that loved him unconditionally and wanted to know what he was so all fired up about anyway, started to batter her. 'Presumably you want me to go somewhere with you?' she questioned coldly.

'On your own feet or over my shoulder,' he offered tautly.

He wouldn't! He bent down—she decided not to risk it.

Taryn swung her legs round and elegantly stepped out of the car. She decided not to wait but made straight for the entrance. Jake was beside her long before she got to the plate glass doors.

A commissionaire smartly held the door open for them. And Taryn did not have to wonder where they were going. Jake's hand coming to her elbow endorsed the fact that he knew precisely where they were heading.

It did not surprise her that they went straight to the top floor. Though, while her insides were madly churning to know what this was all about, she had no wish to be given a humiliating dressing-down in front of Kate.

'I—' Taryn started to protest. But she found that she need not have worried because, with his hand once again on her elbow, Jake guided her straight past the door of the office she had shared with Kate, and along the corridor to the next-door office that was his own.

By that time Taryn had begun to feel well and truly antagonistic to this lofty swine who had ushered her into his office and closed the door. They were at the opposite end of his office, away from his desk, where the sofa and easy chairs were.

'Take a seat,' he clipped.

'It's going to take that long?' she challenged.

He tossed her an unappreciative look for her remark. '*This*,' he grated, 'is where you belong.'

Taryn stared at him, wide-eyed in her surprise. 'H-here?' she stammered. But swiftly got herself together to charge, 'Why are you so angry?'

'You're enough to make a saint angry!' he slammed straight back.

'Well, nobody's ever likely to confuse you with one of those!' she retorted. Oh, my word, that hadn't gone down well!

'Less of the lip,' he ordered curtly.

He was on a hiding to nothing there. She might love him with every part of her being, but it just wasn't in her to stand there and take that sort of talk.

'Huh!' she scorned, though hoped she sounded more brave than she felt, especially when she saw his hands bunch threateningly at his sides. 'So what have I done that's so very terrible?' she asked quickly—a shade less cockily, it had to be said.

'You have the temerity to ask?'

'I—' she tried to get in.

'You have the gall to go back and work for Mellor when—'

'*That* is what it's about?' she gasped, staggered. 'You're angry because—'

'You work for *me* not *him*!' Jake thundered. 'You work *here*, not *there*!'

'But—but you dismissed me!' Taryn exclaimed. Oh, heavens, was there a chance she could come back?

'I did nothing of the kind!' Jake stated flatly. And, when she just stared at him in disbelief, 'When did I?' he demanded.

'You know when!' she retorted, feeling warm suddenly, and not keen to remind him that it had been the morning after she had spent thrilling moments in his arms.

'No, I don't know when,' he denied. 'What did I say to give you such an erroneous impression?'

'Erroneous?' she queried. 'How else was I supposed to interpret it when you said you didn't need me as much as you had thought you did?'

'You thought—' He broke off, but some of his anger seemed to have left him. 'I was—annoyed with you,' he admitted. 'But…'

'You were awful to me!' she exclaimed, and saw more of his mighty anger drain away.

'I was—feeling—um—a bit out of sorts, I suppose,' he reluctantly owned.

'That has to be the understatement of the year.'

'How else was I supposed to be? I've got my pride too, you know.'

'What has pride got to do with it?' she questioned, wishing she'd taken up his offer to take a seat. Now that he was sounding more reasonable, her love for him was rising up and trying to swamp any chance of her opposing him, should he start to get all sharp with her again.

'You'd just as good as told me that in the cold light of day you considered it offensive that the previous evening I'd wanted to make love with you.'

She went red. It had been a foregone conclusion. 'I didn't… I mean, I didn't mean… Oh, grief!' she exclaimed, and, because she really needed the solidity of that sofa beneath her, and he had after all offered, 'Do you mind?' she asked, indicating the sofa with the spread of her hand.

'Please do,' Jake agreed, and as she sat down he took the chair opposite her. But his expression was severe again when, leaning forward, his grey eyes steady on her dark blue ones, 'Are you still in love with Brian Mellor?' he demanded sharply.

Taryn looked back at him. She had thought this was some kind of business discussion, employer to employee—would be, hopefully, employee. But where did Brian and her feelings for him come into it?

'What's that got to do with anything?' she queried. She saw that pulse, that muscle, jerk in Jake's temple again—for all the world as if her question and what he said next put him under some sort of stress.

'It's—got everything to do with everything,' he answered after some moments, as if having to choose his words very carefully.

She couldn't see it. So changed tack to ask outright that which she wanted to know the answer to. 'Are you—um—offering me my old temporary job back?'

'Are you saying you'd be happy to leave Mellor?' Jake asked, and seemed never more tense.

Taryn hesitated. How to answer? If she said she would happily leave Brian—Jake wasn't to know she had already left—might that not imply that she would be more than happy to return to work for Jake? The last thing she wanted this clever man in front of her to pick up was even the smallest clue to how ecstatically happy it would make her to be able to see him every working day.

But Jake had waited long enough for her to answer, it seemed, and was apparently impatient suddenly. Because, before she could formulate the careful words she needed, he was there again, this time stating, 'You walked out on Mellor because he gave you a lover's kiss. You walked out on me, I think I'm beginning to see, because I did the same thing.' He paused, before going steadily on, 'But you went back to Mellor. So now I'm asking—what are my chances of you coming back to me?'

Her heartbeats, that had been having a fine old time within her ever since she had seen Jake in that lift, started to act up again. Jake was sounding as if he really, really wanted her back! How marvellous was that! She wasn't imagining it, was she?'

'You want me to come back?' she asked, nervous in case she had got it wrong.

'Of course,' he answered crisply.

Joy burst in her. She was still going to have to watch that he did not guess at her feelings for him. But, joy of joys, she would see him every day!

Taryn got to her feet. Jake, his eyes never leaving her face, did the same. She tried to sound casual, but her voice was more than a little husky when she said, 'I'll be here at nine on the dot on Monday, then, if that will suit.'

Jake drew a long breath. 'That will suit,' he agreed, and she made to step past him towards the door on her way out. But Jake stepped in front of her and prevented her from leaving. 'Just a minute!' he halted her sharply.

She looked up into his dear, wonderful face and could hardly breathe he was so dear to her. 'Sorry,' she managed to apologise. 'I thought we'd finished our business discussion.'

'That's true. We have. But I haven't finished,' he clipped. 'Not by a long way.'

'Oh!' she murmured, but suddenly thought she saw what he was getting at. 'Should I go and say hello to Kate?'

'Kate isn't in. She has an antenatal appointment.'

'Oh,' Taryn murmured again. 'How's Abby?' Perhaps he was taking her to task for her neglect to mention his step-niece.

'Abby is now fully recovered,' Jake replied, going on, 'And, before you ask, my brother-in-law has benefited from his holiday and my sister is fine.'

'You're being sarcastic.'

'You're being evasive.'

'I'm n...' Not, she'd meant to say. But, 'What I am, is nervous,' was what she blurted out.

'Of me?' he queried, and did not look at all happy when, searching for reasons, 'Sexually, you mean?'

Make me go red again, why don't you! But, no matter how much she did not want him to guess at the love she had for him, it was perhaps because of that love that she could not allow him to think he worried her, made her nervous, in that area. 'No,' she answered. He must know that anyway—it wasn't she who had called a halt to their lovemaking. 'Not that. It's just that...' She stumbled in her search for the right words, fully aware that her face must be scarlet.

'What, Taryn?' he asked quietly. 'Can you not tell me?'

'Y-you make me nervous because—because I don't know what you want from me,' she ended in a rush. 'You said you hadn't finished, not by a long way. But—but if you've done with discussing business, and...and it doesn't look as if you want to discuss Kate or Abby, then—' She broke off, struggling.

'If it's none of those, then it must be personal,' he inserted. 'Personal between you and me, Taryn.'

Her eyes shot wide. Oh, heavens. She glanced to the door as though seeking to escape. Jake's hand coming to her arm stilled her.

'I—er—don't think I really want to discuss "personal",' she stated, panicking wildly and striving not to show it.

'Why not?' he asked mildly. 'You don't think we've been—sufficiently close to be able to talk "personal"?'

Oh, my stars—she'd be a nervous wreck in a minute. 'I don't want this discussion,' she informed him as firmly as she was able.

'My—you really *are* nervous,' he noted, his eyes assessing, speculative as to the reason.

'It isn't necessary,' she carried on. 'It's not about work, so...'

'In my view, it's vitally necessary,' Jake contradicted.

'You m-mean you want to—um—clear the air of—er—anything personal that's—er—happened between us so that we can get back to a purely business relationship?' she guessed, feeling a little hurt, even though she could see the logic of her never being in his arms again. She took a shaky breath. 'Consider it cleared,' she said, taking a step to go around him and so to the door. 'I'll be here Monday—business as usual.'

His hand on her arm checked her from going anywhere. She realised she should have guessed that it would not be that easy to avoid the discussion that Jake seemed to have set his mind on. Honestly, he need not have bothered—she was hardly likely to take advantage of the fact that she had been near enough naked, had seen him near enough naked, had kissed him, tasted him... Oh, heavens above, stop! Stop it, Taryn! She went to take another step around him, her sights on the door, but Jake, his hand still on her arm, turned her squarely in front of him.

'Are you still in love with Mellor?' he demanded to know.

'Why's that so important?' she asked, a little hostilely she had to admit. Jake had asked her that same question not so very long ago.

'Are you intending to marry him?' He asked another question, his voice taut, his words clipped.

Taryn's lips parted in surprise. Then she recalled how Abby had told Jake that Brian was getting a divorce. And, for a moment just then, Taryn felt that Brian would make a very good smokescreen for her true feelings.

'As yet he hasn't asked me.'

Jake did not care for her answer. 'You'd consider any proposal he made?'

Never, ever! 'I'll let you be the first to know!' Jake's hold on her arm tightened. Oh, my word, that hadn't gone down well.

'Presumably he kissed you again?' Jake challenged gruffly.

'As a matter of fact I didn't wait for him to kiss me. I kissed him,' she replied, recalling the way she had recently ended her working relationship with Brian.

'The devil you did!' Jake snarled. 'A lover's kiss?' he questioned grimly. She recoiled at the very idea, her mouth forming an instinctive no. For her sins, Jake, with everything about him alert, had seen it, and before she had chance to lie and tell him, yes, it *had* been a lover's kiss, he was shrewdly muttering, 'There's something fishy here,' and she realised that she must have looked a shade guilty—evasive, as he had suggested. At any rate, he had spotted that something was not quite true, and was straight in to ask, 'Is there perhaps a lie sticking there in your throat?' But then, quite to her surprise, a hint of a smile appeared about his mouth, and he gave her arm a small shake and enquired, 'Are you going to come clean, Miss Webster? Or…' a devilish light was totally unexpectedly there in his eyes '…or am I going to have to kiss the truth out of you?'

Taryn took a quick step back. 'A fate worse than death!' she exclaimed, although suddenly her lips were twitching, and, realising she had no hope of avoiding the issue—she folded. 'If you must know…' she began.

'The floor is yours,' he invited.

'If you must know—I… Well, I told Brian, when I saw him a week ago—when I was with Abby—that I'd give him a ring. I remembered that on Monday, when you didn't want me—er…' Grief, she felt her colour rise again! 'Anyhow, I didn't think I had a job here any more.' She was starting to get confused. 'And I like to be busy…'

'You rang him and he offered you your old job back?'

'That wasn't why I rang him,' she said, her confusion clearing. ' It was more because I said I'd ring.'

'And because you still love him?' Jake put in, once more sounding short-tempered.

Taryn—Jake her boss or no—gave him an exasperated look. 'That's irrelevant!' she snapped shortly. 'Yes, he offered me my old job back. But, no, I didn't take it.'

'You didn't? What were you doing there today if—'

'I was leaving,' she found she was divulging. 'I'd only gone in for a few days to help out. Since I left Brian's had a bit of a problem in getting the right PA,' she explained. 'The PA he's got now seems fine, but there was a bit of a backlog and… Anyway, today was my last day.'

Jake assimilated that in no time flat, and went on to other matters. 'But he didn't kiss you?'

'Not once. And it was totally out of character when he—um— kissed me before. Poor Brian,' she said softly. 'He's so unhappy. He loves his wife very much, only she's got somebody new. I kissed his cheek when I said goodbye to him today—and no, I don't love him. I just feel so sorry f—'

'You've fallen out of love with him?' Jake cut in, a smile breaking.

His smile made her smile too. 'I was never in love with him,' she confessed, Jake's smile sending her totally off guard for a moment.

'You said you were,' he reminded her abruptly.

'I know. And I thought I did love him. I admire him tremendously. He's such a good and kind person, and—'

'But it wasn't love?' Jake cut in, apparently not interested in hearing a list of her ex-employer's virtues.

'I'm very fond of him,' she replied, but had to agree. 'But, no, it was never love.'

Jake studied her, looked deep into her dark blue eyes, then, 'How do you know?' he asked softly. 'How do you know it was never love?'

Taryn began to panic. 'I just know,' she answered faintly, knowing she had to guard with all she had against him finding out that the true reason was because only since knowing him did she know what being truly in love felt like.

But, 'How do you know?' Jake insisted, when she had no intention of letting the smallest unwary word slip. 'Do you know it's the real thing—real, genuine love—when you look at that other person sometimes and feel as if your heart is going to stop?' His eyes were fixed on hers, refusing to let her look away. 'Do you know you've been so completely captured by this thing that has you in its thrall because when that other person walks into the room your heart starts to pound so loud you fear they might hear it?'

'Oh, Jake!' she gasped, not knowing quite where she was, other than that Jake was describing how she had been so very much affected.

'Do you know yourself a prisoner to this feeling, this emotion, that crept up on you when you were all unsuspecting when, waiting for that person, you feel sick in your heart, in your whole body, when time passes—and of your love there is no sign?'

'Jake,' she mourned, loving him, knowing he was hurting, but— even with no idea why he was opening up to her like this—wanting to help him, her love, if she could.

'And do you know that murderous sensation, that raging jealousy—when previously you didn't know you'd a jealous bone in your body—when your love is merely chatting, laughing, or daring to date anybody, daring to date absolutely anybody, but you?'

Memories, unwanted memories, of his women-friends Louise Taylor and Sophie Austin threw spiteful darts at her. Yes, she knew about jealousy. 'Oh, Jake,' she said softly. 'You love her like that? You love her so much?' Taryn did not want him to love anyone but her. But, since that was never going to happen, she could not help but feel his pain.

'More than that,' he admitted. 'She rules my head, scrambles my brain, so that sometimes I can't even think straight because of her.'

He had no idea how wounding his words were. But it suddenly came to her that Jake must be hurting unbearably to be sharing this with her. She had always thought of him as a very private man. While she supposed she should be flattered that he should share with her the depths of his feelings for his love, she was stunned too that he should trust her so.

'Doesn't she—doesn't she love you?' Taryn asked, bleeding a little inside and trying hard to stamp down on those waves of jealousy that were now insisting on pounding her. 'Doesn't she return your feelings?' she pressed on. Jake was looking at her, his eyes never seeming to leave her face, and she had the weirdest feeling all at once that she was missing something here. 'I m-mean,' she went on, feeling nervous all of a sudden, 'have you asked her how she feels? Have you told her how *you* feel?'

Jake already had hold of one of her arms. He brought his other hand up to her other arm. And, holding her there steady, his grey eyes looking intently into her dark blue eyes, 'What the devil do you think I've been trying to do this past half-hour but tell her?' he replied shatteringly.

Her mouth went dry. She couldn't even swallow. He—he couldn't have been speaking about *her!* About his feeling *for her?* No! He... They... And yet... Taryn blinked, rocked on her feet. She couldn't believe it! She stared up at him—Jake held her steady. He had said his love had scrambled his brain—hers seemed to have stopped working altogether. He couldn't be saying what she *thought* he was saying. He couldn't! But—but—jolted though she was, she was the only person he had been talking to this past half-hour!

'M-me?' she queried faintly—and waited for him to collapse laughing. Only he didn't.

He did not collapse laughing. But, his grip on her arms firm still, 'You,' he confirmed.

It was not enough. She needed more. Now she was swallowing, swallowing hard. 'Er—forgive me for appearing a little dense—but—um—are you saying…?' She took a gulp of breath—it was still on the cards that he would laugh his head off. 'Are you saying that *you* are in love—with *me*?'

He did not laugh, and her eyes were riveted on him. Very deliberately, she saw him nod in acknowledgement of his feelings for her. 'I love you so much, Taryn Webster,' he clearly stated. 'I've been near off my head with it.' Utterly dumbfounded, her face flushing and then draining, her insides wild within her, all Taryn was capable of was to look back at him stunned. He was still holding her steady, but did not seem so steady himself as he asked, 'Um—do you think you could ease some of my turmoil by giving me some sort of hint about how you feel about me?'

Taryn hesitated. 'You—don't know?' she asked shakily, the closest she could come just then to making a complete fool of herself.

'Sometimes I've wondered,' he replied. 'Sometimes in my darkest moments I've recalled the way you would have given yourself to me. You wouldn't have gone that far—not with just anybody. I knew that. It was, had been, an especial time for you—that first time. So I had to ask, in those desperately dark moments, was *I* special to you?'

What could she say? She recalled a time when she'd so wanted to be special to him—still did—and here he was asking… She took a deep breath. If she was going to end up with her pride in tatters, so be it. Taryn felt on the brink of a discovery—a discovery that was far more important than pride.

'You—um—are,' she owned huskily.

'Special to you?' he questioned determinedly, as if he needed to hear much more than she had so far revealed.

Taryn, her heartbeats drumming, stared at him amazed. It seemed unbelievable to her that a man she had only ever known as a man who was sure about everything should be so unsure about her.

'I'd have said—extraspecial—to me,' she murmured.

'You love me?'

'Oh, yes, Jake Nash, I love you,' she replied, and felt so full of emotion just then she did not know whether she was going to laugh or cry.

'My darling!' His uncertainty was replaced by a heartfelt smile, and tenderly Jake drew her into his arms, holding her close up against him. A few moments later he pulled back so he could see into her face. 'Say it again,' he demanded.

She loved him, adored him. He was her world. 'I love you—am in love with you. And will you pinch me, please, so that I can believe that this is really happening and I'm not in the middle of some wonderful dream?'

'I can do better than that,' he said softly, and his head came down and—bliss of bliss—his lips met hers.

Taryn did not know quite where she was when at last Jake pulled back. She smiled shyly at him, he smiled right back. 'When?' she asked, her heart full to bursting. 'When did you know?'

'Of my feeling for you?' Jake kissed her again, and seemed to understand that his declaration of love was so new to her, she needed to hear more—her confidence needed more.

He looked lovingly into her face and had to kiss her again and seemed as though he never wanted to stop kissing her. And, when she would not have minded in the least, he looked into her eyes, and as if prepared to do whatever he had to, so she should have belief in his love for her, he moved her to sit with him on the sofa.

With his safe and secure arm about her shoulders, 'How, when, why did I fall in love with you?' He asked the question she was asking.

'Please,' she answered.

'I adore you,' he murmured, for all the world as if he could not prevent the words from leaving him—not now, not now that he knew that his feelings for her were returned. Again he looked as though he might break off to kiss her. But, recollecting that Taryn needed to know of his love, he did not hold back from revealing, 'I first saw you that day you walked out on Mellor. You bolted before I could find out more, and I, to my surprise, realised I *wanted* to find out more. I, in actual fact, returned to the building several times, on the off-chance of seeing you again.'

'You didn't?' she gasped.

'Trust me—when I could quite easily have sent someone else— I decided I had better go myself.'

'You couldn't have been in love with me then?'

'Something was happening. Something I wasn't recognising other than perhaps a passing interest in an upset young woman,' Jake replied. 'But I couldn't forget you. So you can imagine my immense surprise when I go to check that my great uncle Osgood isn't being exploited by his temporary housekeeper, to find that the paragon of virtue he has been talking about is none other than my girl in the lift.'

'You recognised me,' she recalled.

'Instantly!' Jake smiled a wonderful smile. 'You had been popping up in my head from time to time. I left my uncle that day knowing that his daughter had nothing to worry about. Then,' he continued, 'two events coincided. You would soon be leaving my uncle, and Kate told me of her pregnancy. She'd been suffering for some weeks, so I felt I should not only get cover for her but get that person in to help her sooner rather than later…'

'You thought of me?'

'How could I not?' Jake answered tenderly, a world of love there in his tone. 'There was just something about you. While I admit I'd never interviewed anyone who'd reacted in quite the way you did, I couldn't help feeling, rightly or wrongly, that it had to be you.'

She sighed, and wanted to kiss him. 'So you took me on,' she prompted.

'For my sins,' he teased. 'I had always enjoyed my work—

coming to my office. But I had the first inkling that I might have a problem when I suddenly discovered that I was enjoying coming into the office more than ever, and that I looked forward to hearing you come in.'

'Oh,' she sighed blissfully.

'What I didn't like—as you found out—was that men like Robin Cooper, Kenton Harris and Franco Causio should ask you out. And who the devil was this Matt who you greeted so delightedly when he phoned? I confess, my lovely Taryn, I wanted you to greet me the same way when I rang you at the office.'

She stared at him. If it was truly a dream, she never wanted to wake up. 'I don't think you ever did ring,' she remarked, her head and her heart full to bursting.

'Heartless woman! I rang from Italy, hoping it would be you and not Kate who answered the phone.'

Taryn straight away then recalled that day. 'Kate had gone home,' she remembered. 'But you said you wanted to speak to her.'

'I could hardly say I was having a soft-in-the-head moment,' Jake replied with a grin.

'Soft in the head?' she murmured lovingly.

'I'm afraid so. I was missing you—even if I wasn't yet ready to acknowledge what was happening to me.'

'You were falling in love with me?'

'Oh, yes, sweet Taryn. I was. Why else would I come straight from the airport here the very next day?'

Taryn had an idea she might have gone a delicate shade of pink. 'You called in—and I was using your shower.'

His grin was delicious. 'Oh, so you were. By then I was aware of your dedication to duty. If you'd been working without Kate that day too, there was a good chance you might have been working late to clear everything up for the weekend. But—' his grin became positively wicked '—you weren't bent over your computer.'

'Don't remind me!'

'I fear I shall—often,' he tormented. She laughed, she loved him. 'Then I took you to Italy with me—and found I was feeling quite put out when you refused to have dinner with me.'

'I regretted so much saying I wasn't hungry that night,' she confessed.

'You—*wanted* to have dinner with me?'

'I think I was feeling very mixed up about you,' she admitted.

'Good,' he answered. 'Is that why you were so anti on the flight home?'

'If I remember rightly, you could have taught a bear with a sore head a thing or two.'

Jake accepted that. 'I lived to regret it,' he answered with charm, and thrilled her by revealing, 'I was checking things through at home the next day, when all at once I had to give in to the feeling of wanting to see you again.' He gave a wry smile. 'It just wouldn't wait until Monday. Little did I know, though, when I rang you to come to my home to check details on that contract, that I would see you at the Irwin that night.'

Her confidence was growing and growing, and she just had to laugh as she reminded him, 'You were supposed to be at the Raven!'

He kissed her—it seemed he just had to—and disclosed, 'I'd got you to book that table thinking to give someone a call...'

'Louise, or Sophie, or—'

'Tell me you were jealous.'

'I was jealous,' she obliged.

Jake laughed delightedly and kissed her again. 'So, because of you, I was starting to find I was not too interested in other women all of a sudden. I cancelled the reservation and attended a semi-business dinner, anticipating I would be in for something of a dull evening.' He gently stroked a hand down the side of her face. 'Imagine my surprise when I saw you there.'

'You couldn't have been any more surprised than I was to see you,' Taryn answered, and had to grin when he did.

'It wasn't too long, though, before the fact that you're pretty smart when it comes to temp work came in extremely useful.'

'Abby?'

'Abby,' he agreed. 'You being in my home was supposed to ease a load of anticipated problems. What I hadn't foreseen was that you being there would throw up much more trouble than your presence solved.'

'I thought Abby was quite good!' Taryn exclaimed. 'And in all fairness the poor girl couldn't help being unwell.'

'Abby,' he replied, 'was a piece of cake. You, on the other hand, my little darling, were the problem.'

'Me! What did I do?'

'You, sweetheart, made me fall in love with you. I knew it that night you moved in. That night I could deny it no longer. That night I no longer wanted to deny it. In fact, I could not have denied it even had I tried.'

'Oh,' she murmured ecstatically.

'Oh is right,' Jake said, shaking his head. 'All I wanted to do was to take you in my arms, to hold you, to hold you close.'

How absolutely heart-racingly wonderful it was to hear him say so. 'From—er—memory, I believe you did manage to do that when Abby was about.'

'I cheated,' he confessed. 'On one particular occasion she was long gone when I just had to hold on to you.'

'Jake Nash, for shame!' she scolded him laughingly.

'Well, what's a man to do? I wanted to be alone with you, but never seemed to get the chance. There always seemed to be somebody around,' he excused. He kissed her long and tenderly, and was forgiven his sins. 'I've missed you, my darling,' he breathed.

'Me too,' she whispered, and they kissed again, and held each other. 'Oh, Jake,' she whispered. 'I'm so glad we bumped into each other today.' She kissed him in enchantment. But then asked, a little horrified, 'If we hadn't met today we might never have known—'

'There was no chance of our never meeting again,' he cut in, and sounded totally positive about that.

'There wasn't?'

Jake kissed the tip of her nose and let go of her for a few seconds, to put a hand inside his pocket. He withdrew an envelope and showed it to her. It was addressed to her in his firm handwriting.

'I've been carrying this around since Tuesday,' he said. 'Each time I've been halfway to your home, to deliver it in person, fear that it might all backfire on me has made me change my mind. But I doubt I would have lasted the weekend without paying you a call.'

'You've written me a letter?' Taryn asked amazed.

'Not so much a letter,' Jake replied with a crooked kind of grin. 'I discovered I have nerves too, where you're concerned. It's more an official reminder that you are expected to give me a month's notice to resign your employment with me.'

She had to smile. 'Official, but not typed by Kate—handwritten by you.'

'I needed a point of contact,' he confessed, going on, 'I was hoping if I could get you to come back for a month…'

'That we…?'

'Would talk, discover—that I might find out if I had a chance,' he took up, and was never more serious when, 'Taryn Webster,' he went on, 'I love you to complete and utter distraction. So what,' he asked, 'are we going to do about it?'

Anything at all he said would be fine by her.

'What do you suggest?'

'Well, it's for certain we can't go on the way we have been.'

'We can't?'

He shook his head. 'I've been aware of a couple of occasions when I've overstepped the mark in our relationship in the office—' He broke off, and with a self-deprecating look said, 'I couldn't believe I'd kissed you that day I apologised when my jealousy over Kenton Harris got the better of me.'

'It was a very nice apology,' she said demurely, an imp of mischief in her eyes.

Again Jake claimed her lips. It was a very satisfying kiss. 'Where was I?' he asked, drawing back to feast his eyes on her.

'You think I can remember?'

Jake laughed. 'You haven't told me yet when you knew of your feelings for me,' he reminded her. 'When you knew you loved me.'

'I think it just sort of crept up on me,' she said. 'I knew when I'd been working for you for about a month that I no longer loved Brian Mellor.'

'You said you'd never loved him,' Jake further reminded her—perhaps a tinge jealously.

'I hadn't realised that then—not until later. I think I'd thought myself in love with him for so long it had just become a habit. But I knew where my true feelings lay a week last Monday, when you asked me if I'd move in and help you with Abby.'

'You knew then? You're sure?'

'I couldn't be more sure,' she replied happily.

'Good,' Jake announced. 'Now, I have to tell you, my dear love, that I cannot go through another week of listening for sounds of you arriving next door, and then having to suffer the unbearable sickness that has battered me when I've had to accept that you were not coming.'

'So I'm to come in on Monday?'

'As a temporary measure,' he agreed. But she had known the job was temporary anyway. 'But, since the ethics of the situation rule that I cannot have you in my home, in my bed—' He broke off. 'You have gone a very pretty pink,' he teased, but had put all teasing aside when he went on, 'Sweet love, I can't have you in my home *and* in my office…'

'Is that why you—?' She came to an abrupt stop and felt herself going pink again. But she had his full attention and felt compelled to continue. 'Was that why you didn't—er—we didn't…?'

'Make love that night?' Jake saved her further embarrassment. And when she nodded, 'Dear Taryn,' he said, 'I hadn't declared to you how I felt. I suppose until I had some idea if my love was returned I was more than a little apprehensive about doing so. I've never told any woman I love her—it seemed a bit of a mountain to climb. Anyhow, it suddenly slammed into me that you were a guest in my home—an innocent guest, a guest who was doing me a huge favour with regard to Abby—but with Abby not there, I was taking advantage of the situation we found ourselves in. And if that wasn't enough, on top of all that, we were going to see each other in the office every day—so how were you going to feel if you did not love me but had allowed me to take advantage?'

Good heavens. She knew Jake was used to thinking on his feet. But... 'You thought all that when we were in the middle of...?'

'Not very clearly, I must admit,' he owned. 'But back in my room I spent a long, wakeful night thinking, hoping—and then, as soon as I see you, you round on me, and I suddenly don't know where the hell I am. I'm certainly not prepared to risk dropping my guard and telling you of my love.'

'You'd thought to do that?'

'I'd planned to do just that—and hoped for a favourable response.'

'I—wasn't very nice, was I?'

'I wouldn't say that,' he replied lovingly. 'Let's just say our conversation that morning was very different from the one I'd hoped for. It caused me to feel vulnerable, uncertain. Uncertain isn't what I do. I'm no good at it. It bothers me and seems to bring out the worst in me.'

'Oh, Jake,' she murmured. She just had to kiss him.

'So,' Jake began, looking as though he might return the compliment and kiss her. But apparently he had something building up inside him which he had to have said. 'Having frightened the life out of me when I saw you get into that lift not so long ago...'

'You were frightened?'

'Alarmed, monumentally jealous, outraged, terrified, angry, furious—you name it. I experienced a dozen emotions all in a matter of seconds.'

'Because you thought I'd gone back to work for Brian?'

'Seeing you there seemed to confirm my worst fears. As far as I knew you loved him, and he was getting divorced. He desired you. I got mad—demented. No way were you going to marry the man if I had anything to do with it. And I got furious. How dare you go back and work for him? I got possessive—you were my PA, not his, and I had spent a week listening for you, waiting for you. It was not on. It was very definitely not on, Miss Webster!'

'Oh, Jake,' she sighed. 'What a lovely rant you had—and I reaped the benefit of it.'

'Did I ever tell you I think you're pretty wonderful?'

'Oh, Jake,' she murmured dreamily. 'I— um—happen to think you're pretty wonderful too.'

'That's good,' he breathed, and, his look gentle, his tone tender, 'My sweet darling, what I've been trying to say for the last ten minutes, but I own not making a very successful job of it, is if you want to continue working in my office—and I have to tell you I need you near me all the time—then surely you must see that you'll have to marry me—at the very soonest.'

'Marry you?' she questioned faintly.

'I'm going too fast?'

'N-no. Er, you want me to marry you?' Taryn asked shakily. So much had happened, she didn't know whether she was on her head or her heels.

'Well, I can't have you working here and not be married to you. It wouldn't be at all acceptable,' Jake told her firmly.

'It wouldn't?'

Jake looked only marginally shame-faced as he owned, 'Quite honestly, I'm ready to use any excuse—but I'll settle for nothing less.' And, looking deeply into her eyes, he confessed tenderly, 'I need you to marry me more particularly because I have you in my heart. I love you so much that I shall only ever be happy again if you consent to be my wife.'

'Oh, Jake.' She had to swallow hard before she could tell him, 'I couldn't bear for you to be sad.'

He smiled then, the most heartfelt smile. 'I'll take that as a yes, then, shall I?'

Was there ever any doubt? 'Yes,' she whispered. 'I'd be thrilled, honoured and delighted to be Mrs Jake Nash.'

'Sweet darling!' he breathed in joyous delight—and gathered her close.

0307 Gen Std HB

**MILLS & BOON®**

*Live the emotion*

# APRIL 2007 HARDBACK TITLES

## ROMANCE™

**The Ruthless Marriage Proposal** *Miranda Lee* 978 0 263 19604 7
**Bought for the Greek's Bed** *Julia James*   978 0 263 19605 4
**The Greek Tycoon's Virgin Mistress** *Chantelle Shaw*
978 0 263 19606 1
**The Sicilian's Red-Hot Revenge** *Kate Walker*   978 0 263 19607 8
**The Italian Prince's Pregnant Bride** *Sandra Marton*
978 0 263 19608 5
**Kept by the Spanish Billionaire** *Cathy Williams* 978 0 263 19609 2
**The Kristallis Baby** *Natalie Rivers*   978 0 263 19610 8
**Mediterranean Boss, Convenient Mistress** *Kathryn Ross*
978 0 263 19611 5
**A Mother for the Tycoon's Child** *Patricia Thayer*
978 0 263 19612 2
**The Boss and His Secretary** *Jessica Steele*   978 0 263 19613 9
**Billionaire on her Doorstep** *Ally Blake*   978 0 263 19614 6
**Married by Morning** *Shirley Jump*   978 0 263 19615 3
**Princess Australia** *Nicola Marsh*   978 0 263 19616 0
**The Sheikh's Contract Bride** *Teresa Southwick* 978 0 263 19617 7
**The Surgeon and the Single Mum** *Lucy Clark*   978 0 263 19618 4
**The Surgeon's Longed-For Bride** *Emily Forbes*   978 0 263 19619 1

## HISTORICAL ROMANCE™

**A Scoundrel of Consequence** *Helen Dickson*   978 0 263 19757 0
**An Innocent Courtesan** *Elizabeth Beacon*   978 0 263 19758 7
**The King's Champion** *Catherine March*   978 0 263 19759 4

## MEDICAL ROMANCE™

**Single Father, Wife Needed** *Sarah Morgan*   978 0 263 19796 9
**The Italian Doctor's Perfect Family** *Alison Roberts*
978 0 263 19797 6
**A Baby of Their Own** *Gill Sanderson*   978 0 263 19798 3
**His Very Special Nurse** *Margaret McDonagh*
978 0 263 19799 0

MILLS & BOON®

0307 Gen Std LP

Live the emotion

# APRIL 2007 LARGE PRINT TITLES

## ROMANCE™

**The Christmas Bride** *Penny Jordan*              978 0 263 19439 6
**Reluctant Mistress, Blackmailed Wife** *Lynne Graham*
                                                  978 0 263 19440 X
**At the Greek Tycoon's Pleasure** *Cathy Williams*  978 0 263 19441 8
**The Virgin's Price** *Melanie Milburne*          978 0 263 19442 6
**The Bride of Montefalco** *Rebecca Winters*      978 0 263 19443 4
**Crazy about the Boss** *Teresa Southwick*        978 0 263 19444 2
**Claiming the Cattleman's Heart** *Barbara Hannay*
                                                  978 0 263 19445 0
**Blind-Date Marriage** *Fiona Harper*            978 0 263 19446 9

## HISTORICAL ROMANCE™

**An Improper Companion** *Anne Herries*           978 0 263 19388 8
**The Viscount** *Lyn Stone*                       978 0 263 19389 6
**The Vagabond Duchess** *Claire Thornton*         978 0 263 19390 X

## MEDICAL ROMANCE™

**Rescue at Cradle Lake** *Marion Lennox*          978 0 263 19343 8
**A Night to Remember** *Jennifer Taylor*          978 0 263 19344 6
**The Doctors' New-Found Family** *Laura MacDonald*
                                                  978 0 263 19345 4
**Her Very Special Consultant** *Joanna Neil*      978 0 263 19346 2
**A Surgeon, A Midwife: A Family** *Gill Sanderson* 978 0 263 19537 6
**The Italian Doctor's Bride** *Margaret McDonagh*  978 0 263 19538 4

MILLS & BOON®

# MAY 2007 HARDBACK TITLES

## ROMANCE™

| | |
|---|---|
| **Bought: The Greek's Bride** *Lucy Monroe* | 978 0 263 19620 7 |
| **The Spaniard's Blackmailed Bride** *Trish Morey* | |
| | 978 0 263 19621 4 |
| **Claiming His Pregnant Wife** *Kim Lawrence* | 978 0 263 19622 1 |
| **Contracted: A Wife for the Bedroom** *Carol Marinelli* | |
| | 978 0 263 19623 8 |
| **Willingly Bedded, Forcibly Wedded** *Melanie Milburne* | |
| | 978 0 263 19624 5 |
| **Count Giovanni's Virgin** *Christina Hollis* | 978 0 263 19625 2 |
| **The Millionaire Boss's Baby** *Maggie Cox* | 978 0 263 19626 9 |
| **The Italian's Defiant Mistress** *India Grey* | 978 0 263 19627 6 |
| **The Forbidden Brother** *Barbara McMahon* | 978 0 263 19628 3 |
| **The Lazaridis Marriage** *Rebecca Winters* | 978 0 263 19629 0 |
| **Bride of the Emerald Isle** *Trish Wylie* | 978 0 263 19630 6 |
| **Her Outback Knight** *Melissa James* | 978 0 263 19631 3 |
| **The Cowboy's Secret Son** *Judy Christenberry* | 978 0 263 19632 0 |
| **Best Friend...Future Wife** *Claire Baxter* | 978 0 263 19633 7 |
| **A Father for Her Son** *Rebecca Lang* | 978 0 263 19634 4 |
| **The Surgeon's Marriage Proposal** *Molly Evans* | 978 0 263 19635 1 |

## HISTORICAL ROMANCE™

| | |
|---|---|
| **Dishonour and Desire** *Juliet Landon* | 978 0 263 19760 0 |
| **An Unladylike Offer** *Christine Merrill* | 978 0 263 19761 7 |
| **The Roman's Virgin Mistress** *Michelle Styles* | 978 0 263 19762 4 |

## MEDICAL ROMANCE™

| | |
|---|---|
| **Single Dad, Outback Wife** *Amy Andrews* | 978 0 263 19800 3 |
| **A Wedding in the Village** *Abigail Gordon* | 978 0 263 19801 0 |
| **In His Angel's Arms** *Lynne Marshall* | 978 0 263 19802 7 |
| **The French Doctor's Midwife Bride** *Fiona Lowe* | |
| | 978 0 263 19803 4 |

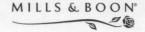

MILLS & BOON®

0407 Gen Std LP

# MAY 2007 LARGE PRINT TITLES

## ROMANCE™

**The Italian's Future Bride** *Michelle Reid*     978 0 263 19447 0
**Pleasured in the Billionaire's Bed** *Miranda Lee*

978 0 263 19448 7
**Blackmailed by Diamonds, Bound by Marriage** *Sarah Morgan*

978 0 263 19449 4
**The Greek Boss's Bride** *Chantelle Shaw*     978 0 263 19450 0
**Outback Man Seeks Wife** *Margaret Way*     978 0 263 19451 7
**The Nanny and the Sheikh** *Barbara McMahon*   978 0 263 19452 4
**The Businessman's Bride** *Jackie Braun*     978 0 263 19453 1
**Meant-To-Be Mother** *Ally Blake*     978 0 263 19454 8

## HISTORICAL ROMANCE™

**Not Quite a Lady** *Louise Allen*     978 0 263 19391 6
**The Defiant Debutante** *Helen Dickson*     978 0 263 19392 3
**A Noble Captive** *Michelle Styles*     978 0 263 19393 0

## MEDICAL ROMANCE™

**The Christmas Marriage Rescue** *Sarah Morgan* 978 0 263 19347 3
**Their Christmas Dream Come True** *Kate Hardy*

978 0 263 19348 0
**A Mother in the Making** *Emily Forbes*     978 0 263 19349 7
**The Doctor's Christmas Proposal** *Laura Iding*   978 0 263 19350 3
**Her Miracle Baby** *Fiona Lowe*     978 0 263 19539 2
**The Doctor's Longed-for Bride** *Judy Campbell*   978 0 263 19540 8